HOME

TO

OBLIVION

By

Roger Whittlesey

Sarah,
Thank you
for reading!

Roger Whittlesey

This book is dedicated to those friends and family members who read my many manuscripts over the years and provided invaluable advice along the way, to my students for eagerly listening to the various versions of the novel, to Caroline and Lee for believing in me, and most of all to Christy, for your constant support and encouragement.

Copyright © 2013 by Roger Whittlesey

First Edition

Whittlesey, Roger
Home To Oblivion/Roger Whittlesey.—1st ed.
ISBN-13: 978-1482745498
ISBN-10: 1482745496

Book design by Roger Whittlesey (all cover images are in the public domain)

Ordering information: This book can be purchased at Amazon.com as both an e-book and a paperback edition.

Chapter One
SAILING

RAFFERTY DOUGLAS CLANGED the ship's bell and hollered, "An English fleet! Portside!"

I peered up at the crow's nest and watched as Edward Taylor fumbled for and then gazed through his small, brass telescope. He then called out, "It's the *Serapis*! And a fleet of smaller vessels!"

Mayhem.

Sailors scurried down the ratlines, rushed up from below deck, and hurriedly set to work preparing the cannons. I stood at the center of this chaotic scene with my back pressed up against the main mast of the *Bonhomme Richard*, a French-made merchant ship turned American warship.

"All hands—man your stations!" yelled Commodore John Paul Jones in a hoarse, powerful voice.

I remained motionless, staring at a small crevice in the starboard bulwark, vainly wishing I were wee enough to crawl into it and hide.

"The convoy of ships has turned!" shouted Edward Taylor, now standing top deck portside. "They are escaping, Commodore!"

"Let them turn," said Jones, dismissively waving his right hand. "It is the *Serapis* that I want."

The turbulent North Sea slapped aggressively against the ship, its dark depths encrusted with yellow-white crests of foam and spray. Above, the slate gray sky was rapidly relinquishing itself to the deathly hues of night.

"Shake a leg, boy! There is plenty to be done," said a slump-shouldered sailor named Mason. "Take this." He thrust a dirk into my hand and then hurriedly limped away to assist his mates along the gunwale. I examined the whalebone handle and the keen point of the knife, and wondered what he expected me to do with it.

My official duty aboard the *Bonhomme Richard* was as an apprentice to Doctor Nathaniel Beckett, but I soon discovered my job responsibilities inclined more toward those of a ship's boy. In my short time at sea, I had mostly labored shoulder-to-shoulder with the illiterate tars—mending sails, pounding oakum into joints of timber, and hauling supplies up from the ship's hold. Though only twelve years old, I stood taller than most of the crew, so naturally the crewmembers, most twice my age, expected from me a man's worth of work. There was no shirking duty during dull times, and now, with battle only moments away, I was expected to toil and die like a man, if death proved to be my destiny.

I can now state without reservation that sailing along England's Flamborough Head on that September evening in 1779, I suddenly felt insufficiently prepared for combat and boundlessly afraid of dying.

"Are you preparing for surgery with that?" said a voice behind me. When I turned around, Edward Taylor smiled and nodded at the whalebone-handled dirk in my hand. "Or are you going to whittle yourself a coffin?" he joked, and then leaned over and picked up two cannonballs.

Taylor was apprenticed as a cooper before the war, not a tailor, as his name would seem to imply. The slightly built sixteen-year-old and I became fast friends in our short time at sea, no doubt gravitating toward each other because of our nearness in age. Taylor was a Connecticut Yankee much devoted to his family and eager to return home to his sweetheart, Constance—he carried with him everywhere a silhouette of her likeness, which he proudly shared with me hours after leaving port.

"Mason handed me this knife," I explained. "What do you suppose I should do with it, I have no . . ."

Bang.

The starboard guns thundered, and then blue-white clouds of gunpowder smoke filled the weather deck. The sailors raced to reload the cannons in preparation for another volley. The British warship, *Serapis*, however, unloaded what seemed like all of its 44 guns at once; cannonballs of different weights and circumferences raced through the air, whistling a tune I soon learned to associate with disfigurement, death, and pain.

The battle pounded on. We took great losses. I watched in horror as a cannonball decapitated a sailor, and then shut hard my eyes as his wriggling, blood-spurting body plunged into the murky North Sea. The sights and sounds of war encircled me: splintering wood, wails of pain, blood-red seawater streaming into the hold, tattered sails, and the deafening boom of cannon fire.

Shouts of distress came from every direction. Men cried out, "Doctor! Over here—hurry!" Amid the pandemonium, I recognized Doctor Beckett by his blue waistcoat, and I rushed to his side to aid him in anyway I could.

Doctor Beckett had to make snap decisions about where to spend his energies. He ordered those men who came to him with only superficial wounds back to their duties. The good doctor instantly prioritized the more serious injuries—detached and severely broken limbs, blunt force trauma to the head, wounds to the chest—as "likely fatal" and therefore did not bother providing medical care. Once, as I tended to a man who had been struck in the chest by a cannonball, the white bone of his ribcage exposed through his ripped and bloody uniform, Doctor Beckett gently tugged at my collar and said, "We cannot waste precious time, Prescott, tending to wounds that will not heal." A dozen or more men, after fifteen minutes of the battle, lay uncared for—convulsing hideously, twitching, shallow breathing, and then, mercifully, dying.

Later, after a piece of shrapnel struck Jonathan Pierce in the leg, Doctor Beckett immediately went to work removing the metal shard. Pierce, the ship's cook, howled miserably as Doctor Beckett probed his calf with metal tweezers. During this and other similar procedures, my job was to stand behind the patient and hold down the arms to protect the doctor from being injured by flailing limbs or purposeful angry attacks. Pierce initially resisted fiercely, but as the pain spiked through his body, he lost consciousness, and restraint became unnecessary. When Doctor Beckett finally extracted the bloody metal fragment, he drew it close to his eyes, examined it, and then, seemingly unimpressed, nonchalantly discarded it over his right shoulder with a flick of the wrist.

The cook's calf appeared like ground beef as the doctor hastily stitched the wound. This gruesome vision caused me to feel lightheaded. On the precipice of fainting, my ears rang and the room swam. I staggered a few steps away and turned my head so that I vomited without splattering the good doctor and the cook. My stomach purged, I soon regained my legs and composure, and moved up to the weather deck in search of men in need of care.

The *Bonhomme Richard* withstood the *Serapis'* hurricane-like force, and then came the eye of the storm. All was suddenly calm. I again heard the familiar creaking of the wooden planks rocking on the tide and the whipping and snapping of the canvas sails filling and flagging in the fickle breezes. Of course, I also heard wheezing lungs, sickening moans, and the agonized screams of the suffering.

"Doctor Beckett!" yelled the first mate. "Young Taylor has been hurt badly." He pointed to a body laying facedown on the deck, metallic rubble strewn about him.

I rushed to my friend and carefully turned him onto his back. I recognized agony and fear in his eyes. "You will be all right," I remember saying over and over, as I peered down at his mangled body. Edward grasped my arm and tried to speak. His green eyes strained, bulged hideously in their sockets. His face underwent transformations of color—from ruddy red, to a sickly greenish hue, then alabaster—deathly pale. I watched as his trembling lips struggled to form words, then his grip weakened, and his hand dropped to the deck. His throat gurgled and his heaving chest ceased moving.

"Prescott, over here!" yelled Doctor Beckett.

I reached down and gently closed Edward Taylor's eyes—shut those intelligent green eyes forever—and then loped over to where the good doctor tended to a wounded man.

The *Bonhomme Richard* was in terrible condition. I overheard a sailor shout, "We are taking on water!" Then the main mast splintered and crashed to the deck, just a few feet from where Jones stood.

"Have you struck your colors?" Admiral Pearson yelled from the deck of the *Serapis*, which had been purposely lashed to our ship with grappling hooks to eliminate the swift ship's forte of maneuverability, and was therefore within shouting distance.

Commodore Jones, his boots stomping in huge strides along the main deck, raised his fist in the air and ordered each man to ready himself for the counterattack. "Struck our colors? Never! The *Serapis* has not seen what we are made of! Sir, we have not yet begun to fight!"

The crew rallied: there was movement again on the deck, and soon our siege guns pounded out new rhythms. Flashes of brilliant light offset the darkness, as the guns and grenades did their deadly duties.

I do not know the exact circumstances that led to my sudden fall overboard, but I do remember the stern side railing giving way beneath me as a great force hit my body from behind. I plummeted into the cold North Sea, and then screamed for help as I desperately swam back toward the *Bonhomme Richard*. But, in the disorienting darkness and the heaving swells, swimming became difficult, and I lost sight of the ship. I was forced to float on my back, rising and falling on the great dark waves, rapidly drifting away from the battle.

At that moment, I was certain my destiny was an underwater grave.

But there was nothing grave in what I found.

Chapter Two
DRIFTING

WHEN SOMETHING IN THE WATER brushed up against my head, I spun around onto my stomach and discovered an eight-foot piece of flotsam that could bear my weight and allow me to rest. I clung to this wooden mass for hours, bobbing on the waves; the whole time cursing my bad luck and speculating about what shape my imminent death would soon take. Would I drown? Would I starve? Would I become dehydrated? Would sharks consume my flesh?

As the sun began to rise, I inspected the surface of the great piece of driftwood to which I clung. Dark and pitted with age, consisting of several boards joined together, I concluded it was a small piece of a once larger construction. In the increasing light I noticed worn, golden lettering on its surface; however, I did not immediately decode it. It began with a capital "J," written in cursive. Next, two letters swam together like waves, followed by "I-P-E-R." There was a space and then a faded character, followed by two more letters that blended together, and a piece of another letter that ended abruptly at the jagged edge.

I pressed my face closer to the inscription and focused my mind on nothing other than the solution to the mystery words. And for a brief time, I dwelled not about the likelihood of becoming a skeletal relic on the ocean floor.

"J . . . I PER," I said, aloud.

The mysterious letters that swam together in both words appeared to be the same, but they were faded and obscured under a thin layer of seawater. I shifted my weight on the board, brushed away the seawater with my hand, and concentrated more intently on deciphering the undulating shapes.

They could be "Ws" or a stretched out letter "Ns." Then I realized it was a "U" followed by an "N," a letter whose shape was actually a "U" turned upside down—capsized.

"JUNIPER," I said. "...UN."

The faded first letter in the second word was either a "B," a "Z," or an "S."

"JUNIPER SUN . . . something," was what I finally settled on. "What is a Juniper Sun?" I asked myself.

As if I spoke the words Moses had used to part the Red Sea, the waves around me responded with sudden turbulence, and in a matter of minutes I found myself clinging to the driftwood with all my remaining strength. The heaving, perturbed sea seemed to plot against me, eager to separate me from the wooden board. I plunged downward suddenly from the apex of an angry wave and lost my grip on the board. Another wave enveloped me and I was submerged, tossed about savagely in the roiling surge.

I swam a few strokes beneath the chaotic surface, and then came up for air. When I burst out into the sunlight, I found myself amidst ferociously pounding white-capped breakers. The waves violently flung my body in every direction. One moment I was beneath the waves, the next I was above desperately trying to gather a breath of air. And, just as my body could not take anymore, I touched ground, though the tide continued to trip me. Each time I submerged, the roar of the waves became instantly muffled, and I would have felt as if I had re-entered the comfort of the womb if it were not for the terror of fearing I may never breathe again.

Then, in one final moment of brutality, the tide thrust my body over a bed of stones and onto a sandy shore. Fearful another wave would drag me back into the sea, I quickly scampered on all fours to a higher spot on the beach. I lay there several minutes and caught my breath. Then I weakly rose to my feet and had a look around.

Sprawled out in front of me was what I presumed to be an island—tropical and mountainous—with a great volcanic peak at its center.

Chapter Three
GLITTERING

BLACK SMOKE GENTLY ROSE from the island's volcanic peak before sluggishly trailing west and then disappearing beyond the horizon. Gazing below the conical volcanic summit, the mountain became sheer; brown and craggy cliffs submerged, from my view on the beach, into giant palm leaves outstretched and basking in the equatorial sun.

Trade winds blew in from the southeast, but provided little relief from the smothering heat. I turned my back to the volcano, bent my knees, and dropped onto the soft sand. Beyond the foaming six-foot waves that crashed vigorously onto the beach, the sea met the sky in every direction. From the vantage point of the gulls circling high above, I imagined I appeared like an inconsequential speck on a land surrounded by a boundless body of water.

Where am I? What have I gotten myself into? I was exhausted, weak, and hungry.

I must begin provisioning. The island would provide coconuts, berries, and sea animals—crabs, squid, fish, and clams—to eat. Perhaps I could hunt game—rabbits, wild pigs, and pheasants—in the jungle beyond the beach.

I stood up, turning my back to the sizzling surf, and focused my eyes on the forest twenty paces away. Large broad leaves hid any interior features of the rain forest, though I surmised that a short walk into the forest would reveal a shady, more comfortable, place to settle.

I glanced down at my feet, shod in a pair of dark leather shoes with square brass buckles, and noticed a familiar configuration of indents next to me in the sand—footprints. Made by an upright biped of considerable size—most likely a human—the biped was barefoot, which I inferred from the deep heel and toe indentations.

I followed the prints west for several rods until they suddenly disappeared, as if the pedestrian had been lifted in the air, or had climbed up into a tree. I looked up and saw nothing but blue sky intermingled with wisps of black volcanic smoke. Behind me, the surf pounded a bank of coral rock. In front of me, to my surprise, stood two stone, nearly identical, statues—round-bellied children with impish grins, distant eyes, and two loop earrings in one ear. One figure held a granite-carved human skull. The other held a flower. The gray stone had dark streaks running down it from what I surmised was from years of wear and exposure to the weather, sea, and sun. Two paces beyond the statues, dark green leaves hung from coiled vines. I held out my hand the way you do when offering a handshake, fished it through the hanging vines, and then brushed several of the vertical strings of vinery to the side.

The burning sunlight, which applied a nearly palpable weight upon my neck and shoulders, streamed in through the outspread vines and revealed a well-worn trail consisting mostly of hard-packed soil sprinkled with sand. Pedestrians had dragged the sand, I suspected, when walking in from the beach.

I stepped onto the path, letting the whorled vines fall back into their original place. It took a short duration for my eyes to adjust to the darkness, and when they did, I realized that the trail was long and straight—traveling for almost seventy yards before dipping over a hill.

My first temptation was to follow this trail, hopeful that it would lead me to civilization, but fears of unknown dangers overrode this urge. It was quiet in the dusky darkness, now that the occluding vegetation muffled the sound of roaring waves and whistling sea breezes.

No birds sang. No animals stirred in the bushes. I did not even feel the presence of insects slithering and crawling among the soil and leaves, yet I knew that for such a complicated ecosystem to thrive as this one did, all things absent to my senses were, in fact, only hidden from view. Experience taught me that creatures in nature would instantly disappear when danger was near. I had witnessed the forest of New England grow eerily tranquil when a large predatory animal arrived. I wondered if I were being perceived as that large predatory animal, or whether there was something else within proximity that could be construed as one.

The human footprints in the sand had to have been fresh, I conjectured, because any tropical rainstorm would eliminate them, and I knew that such a rainforest as this would not likely pass a day—several hours even—without precipitation. Therefore, I concluded—rather more quickly than it takes to illustrate in written form—that there were humans on the island. Upon making this observation, I began fleshing out my hypothesis. Are they natives of this island? Perhaps they are other survivors of the sea battle. Are they friendly? Are they my political enemy?

I pressed through the vines and walked out onto the warm beach sand. The sunlight beamed down upon my face, soon causing beads of perspiration to form on my skin. Surviving in this heat would be impossible without fresh water; however, I was not concerned about finding a water source because the sprawling vegetation indicated an abundant supply.

To the east, approximately 200 yards away, I noticed a glint of reflected light. The white light blinked off and on—as if in some code. My pulse quickened, as I imagined my anonymity on the isle disintegrating. I also had fears about losing my life, especially if the signaling faction was unfriendly—British. These silver coins of light shot across the beach and deposited in my eyes. It was a message for me, I concluded, and required—demanded—my immediate response.

I began walking toward the flickering light. Travel was easier now that my clothing—long canvas pants, a white cotton shirt, and a blue waistcoat—was nearly dried. Within a hundred yards, I began to make out poles—at least a half dozen of them—sticking upright out of the sand. Only a couple of inches in diameter, the poles were as tall as a man. These shiny signals came, I could now see, from a pole centered within the rest. Something hung from it, something metallic or glass.

I moved away from the shore, near a sheer cliff that rose hundreds of feet above sea level. I walked stealthily along this great natural wall, and then kneeled on the sandy ground when within 10 yards of the poles.

The wind disturbed the metallic object hanging from the center pole and created a jangling sound. I screwed up my courage, scanned the area for other inhabitants—the owners of the poles—and slowly approached the jangling object.

A metallic chain—a necklace chain attached to two rectangular metal plates—hung on a small nub on the wooden pole. Stamped into these half-inch by one-inch-wide plates were English words and numbers. Each plate had the same information. Each read as follows,

THOMPSON
C. D.
620342003   AB
USMC M
PROTESTANT

I gathered the plates into my palm, raised them off the pole, and then placed them in my coat pocket.

"I'm not alone, after all," I said aloud, as I stared out at the barreling waves.

"No—you're not," said a raspy-voiced man in an accent I did not recognize. The man was standing directly behind me.

Chapter Four
ESTABLISHING

I SWUNG AROUND and stood face-to-face with a young man wearing a forest green uniform. The young man, a Caucasian with spectacles resting on his straight nose, smiled broadly, revealing a remarkable set of pearly-white teeth. I surmised he was only a few years older than me, perhaps 16 years old. I stood astonished and unable to produce a word. This strange-looking young man wearing peculiar clothing (trousers with pockets along the sides, calf-high, black leather boots with laces down the front, and a time piece strapped to his wrist) continued to smile, and I soon felt very uncomfortable.

"Welcome to the island, kiddo," he said, keeping his eyes locked on mine. "My name is Caleb Thompson; Private First Class; United States Marine Corps; late of Concord, New Hampshire, yada, yada, yada."

He offered his hand and I shook it. Then he turned his back to me, took several relaxed strides toward the shaded section of the beach, beneath the jutting cliffs, and sat down on the sand, his hands clasped in front of him, his elbows resting on his knees.

"So what about you?" he said in a booming voice. "Why the costume? You an actor?"

I looked down at my waistcoat and canvas pants. There was nothing theatrical about the garments. I wondered if this strange man was jesting.

"Actor?" I uttered selfconsciously as I ran my right hand across the breast pocket of my coat. "Why would you say . . . ? I'm a doctor's apprentice and a ship's boy—at least I was until yesterday."

"A ship's boy, huh," he said, taking out a cigarette, lighting it with a metallic flame producer, and then sucking in the tobacco smoke. "Are you part of a crew on a historical boat? I have a buddy back in New England who worked as a crewman on a tall ship."

"The ship I sailed on is a frigate . . . now a warship."

"Oh," Caleb interrupted, "you were on a battleship—18 inch guns and all." His face changed for a moment; it seemed to indicate that he was satisfied with this information. But then perplexity, furrowed brows, squinted eyes, made a statue of his face.

"Wait a minute," he said, getting to his feet and walking toward me. "You're just a kid. And your accent—British, right?"

"Yes; I suppose I am," I stated hesitantly. "But I should inform you that I am not a loyalist."

"Oh," said Caleb, pulling one of the wooden poles from the ground. "I know where you're coming from."

"You do?" I said, pleased that he knew my origins, and hopeful that he would be able to provide me with directions back. It struck me that I might be home sooner than I thought.

"Yeah," said Caleb. "It's not easy staying loyal when there are protests back at home, people yelling at soldiers, and a feeling that you're fighting a war that no one wants."

"Where I'm from, in Massachusetts Bay Colony, I saw the protests first hand," I explained, as Caleb pulled the remaining poles out of the sand. "After the Intolerable Acts, people changed their views on the Regulars, and I would say that many wanted to avoid a war with England—some remained loyal—but, I think it is an exaggeration to state that no one wants the war."

Caleb's mouth hung open in an exaggerated expression of bewilderment. He dropped six wooden poles to the sand, the cigarette fell from the precarious perch of his bottom lip, and then he seemed to study his boots before shaking his head and starting to laugh.

"Did you say England?" he said in a distant voice; an incredulous airy tenor replaced the booming bass voice. "What, are you a nut?"

"What do you mean?" I suddenly realized that Caleb had been asking all the questions. I suppose, out of politeness, I allowed him to lead the questioning because, after all, I had walked on to his island. However, I had some of the same questions to ask him—about his clothes, his accent (certainly not a New England accent), and his reason for being on this island.

"I get it," said Caleb, with a look of relief on his face. "You're joking with me, right?"

I didn't know what to say. My silence affected his new joviality.

"This is getting stranger by the minute," he said. "Listen . . . what the heck is your name, anyway?"

"Prescott Fielding," I said. "Apprentice to the chief surgeon Nathaniel Beckett on the *Bonhomme Richard*."

Caleb picked up the poles, walked past me, and with the wave of his hand, beckoned me to follow him. We walked east, for nearly a half-mile, before turning toward the center of the island and ascending a fairly precipitous path.

"*Bonhomme Richard*, Regulars, the Intolerable Acts," Caleb said, as he grasped my hand to help me up a particularly difficult section of terrain. "I'm starting to feel like I'm back in tenth grade history with Mr. Egan."

Caleb and I walked in silence for several minutes. In that time, we traveled west and continued—though more slowly—upward. Eventually, we walked on the craggy rock of the cliff that we had stood in the shadow of just 15 minutes earlier. There, imbedded in the leafy landscape, was a shelter—a lean-to composed of wood sticks and roofed with layers of palm leaves over a green tarpaulin. The structure, about seven feet in height, was about 10 feet deep and eight feet wide. Inside the lean-to, Caleb had created a bed consisting of palm leaves, and there was a makeshift table made from a long flat rock that sat upon a small wooden case. Peeking beyond the hooch, which is what Caleb called this structure, I realized there was an eight-foot fissure in the giant rock on which we stood. The fissure plunged fifty or more feet downward. And from what I could discern, there was but only one way to get to Caleb's hut, and that was by walking along the narrow path that we had traversed. Caleb had chosen his site wisely. From atop of this perch, he had a clear view of the ocean, the volcanic mountain, and more than a mile in both directions of the beach.

From this perch Caleb likely saw me as I floundered in the surf, walked onto the beach, and followed the footprints, west, along the upper part of the beach. He must have watched me enter the thick vegetation. Perhaps it was at this time when he descended and arrived on the spot where we met.

Caleb gently placed the poles next to his hut, and then sat on the ground, his back against an elephant-sized stone.

"Sit down, Prescott," he said in that unusual dialect. "We have a lot to talk about." Caleb pointed to a pile of palm leaves next to the hooch. It was a crude cushion—Caleb's seat on this mysterious island.

Seated, I leaned my back against the trunk of a palm tree and felt my body relax, perhaps for the first time since before the battle against the *Serapis*. Caleb reached for a green garment, a shirt of several intermingled greens, browns, and tans, and lifted a pocket, pulling from it a banana, which he then tossed to me. I caught the piece of fruit and thanked him. It was a welcome feeling to place something nourishing into my body. I had not eaten a morsel since breakfast, which I estimated was 10 hours earlier in the day, even though the sun's position in the sky did not agree with this estimate (it stood directly above in its lunchtime seat in the sky).

"Prescott, have you ever heard of the Vietnam Conflict?"

"I'm afraid I have not," I said, somewhat embarrassed.

"Do the names John F. Kennedy or Lyndon B. Johnson ring a bell for you?"

"Ring a bell?"

"You know," Caleb said, gesticulating grandly with his hands. "Do you know—or, rather, are you familiar with these names?"

"No; they do not sound familiar," I said. "Are they friends of yours?"

"No, Prescott, they're not." Caleb's demeanor grew grave.

"Is there something the matter?"

"I'll answer that question in one moment, but please, Prescott, answer this one last question: What year is it?"

"Why—1779," I said.

"Do you know what year it was when I arrived on this island?" Caleb quickly lifted his hand to keep me from responding. He then raised his forefinger. "Keep in mind I arrived only one month ago."

Caleb's awkward delivery, grave and dramatic, concerned me. I clearly understood that the answer to this question would be unusual. So, instead of stating the obvious, that I believed he landed here in 1779, I shrugged my shoulders.

Caleb stared into my eyes and then spoke slowly, meaningfully. "One month ago it was November 3rd, 1968."

Chapter Five
PLATEAU

THAT FIRST HOUR I SPENT WITH CALEB was the most fantastical hour I have ever lived. My body was a tuning fork, struck by the immensity of all that had transpired, and sensations of absolute wonder vibrated throughout my being. I suppose if man were intelligent and cognizant enough to understand his own birth as it took place, he would perceive the grand newness of the event with the same awe that I perceived these events unfolding before me.

And then as I sat there, leaning against that palm tree, atop of those craggy cliffs, the giddiness dissipated and the sobering reality of my circumstances dulled my spirits.

My eyes returned to Caleb, who reclined against a pile of palm leaves. I noticed his large, brown eyes, somewhat hidden in the distorting lenses of his spectacles. He reclined, relaxed and confident, smoking his last cigarette down to the nub. He exhaled a stream of blue smoke and then put the burning white remainder between his thumb and index finger and flicked it over the cliff. Caleb's hands were large and bony. But there was a fluid motion in the way his hands moved—a fluid motion in the way his whole body moved. There was something about how Caleb walked and talked and leaned or crouched that I considered graceful. Perhaps, athletic is a better description. Caleb was a head taller than me, but I wondered if I would grow to be as tall if not taller than him someday. I realized in what a stark contract I was to Caleb, a skinny twelve year old, with straight black hair parted down the middle, pulled and tied back with a ribbon. I had muscle, but it wasn't developed muscle like the anvils that clung to Caleb's arm bones.

Caleb tilted his head back, revealing an oversized Adam's apple that bulged from his thick neck. His chin was devoid of whiskers, and several pimples discolored his forehead.

The afternoon sun beamed down on us, draining me of nearly all my energy. The banana peel that I had placed on the ground was now a shriveled brown strip. The weather would require acclimation. The sun's strength told me that I was near the equator, but I could not reconcile the fact that I had been aboard the *Bonhomme Richard* hours before, because the battle against the *Serapis* had occurred off the coast of England—2,000 miles from the equator!

Caleb cleared his throat. "So, Prescott," he said. "Where do we begin?"

"I suppose you could begin by telling me where I am. Are we on an island?" That last question attached itself to my initial question when I suddenly realized that I had never confirmed that I was marooned on an island.

"I haven't walked along the entire perimeter, but I think it's pretty safe to say that we're on a volcanic island."

"So, you have explored the island?" I said, now straightening my shoulders.

"To a point."

"Where are we?"

Caleb leaned forward. "Your guess is as good as mine. I only live here." Caleb laughed at this last statement, but I did not share his mirth. "I only got here a month ago."

"Are you alone?"

"Not anymore," he said, and then smiled. Again, I could not help marveling at the condition of his teeth—straight, white, and clean. My own teeth were in good condition, meaning that I still had a mouthful, but I had not seen many people his age with such a marvelous set.

"Have you met other people since arriving on the island?" I asked.

"People?" he said. "No—I haven't."

"Does the island have a name?"

"Again, kiddo," Caleb started, and then reached into a green canvas bag that he called his rucksack and pulled out an orange. He displayed the orange with a sweeping motion of his hand and then in a gesture asked if I would like to eat it. I nodded eagerly and then he threw the orange, underhand, into the soft sand in front of me. "As I was saying, Prescott, I don't really know much more about the island than you do."

"You claim to be from the future," I said, now digging into the peel of the orange with my fingernails.

"I don't claim to be—I am," he said. "You claim to be from the past."

"Well," I said, unsure how to answer this, because to me it was the present.

"The 1700s," he said.

"1779," I specified.

Caleb laughed a little—spurts of laughter intermingled with bursts of air from his pursed lips—and then he held his stomach and laughed aloud.

"What is so funny?" I feared that he was laughing at me.

"Oh," he said, between a burst of short laughter, "I just find the whole thing amusing and insane."

"Not me," I said. "I find it to be quite overwhelming." I stood up and stared out at the sea. Where was the *Bonhomme Richard*? Which way was home? Could I ever get home? What if I built a boat? Could I sail off of this island and return to my former life? The questions were seemingly endless, and what frustrated me most was that Caleb knew very little more about our circumstances.

Caleb rose and moved by my side. We stood shoulder-to-shoulder upon that cliff, staring out at the restless sea. Well, perhaps shoulder-to-his elbow is a more accurate description, as my head barely reached the height of his shoulders.

Caleb lifted his left arm and pointed down and left, to the beach below. "That's where I first saw you," he said. "You came stumbling out of the sea and then sat there on the sand."

"What is this all about?" I said, tears welling in my eyes, as an aberrant fear clung to my heart.

Caleb patted me on the back. "I know what you're going through, kiddo," he said. "I do."

"What is going to become of me . . . of us?" I wondered aloud.

"We are going to survive," Caleb said, his voice bursting with an enthusiasm that sounded contrived. "You play the hand that is dealt you, man."

He walked behind me, and then I heard him rifling through his rucksack. When he returned to my side, I noticed he held a knife in his hand with a slightly serrated blade—about 12 inches in length— and a curious green handle.

"What are you doing?" I asked, a little frightened.

"Are you hungry?"

"Yes."

"What do you say we go rustle up some supper, and then, after we've eaten, we can talk about serious things?"

Caleb pushed the blade between his belt and his trousers. He patted me on the back and then began walking toward the narrow trail that we had recently ascended to reach what Caleb called "The Plateau."

"What are we hunting?" I said, now following.

"Dodo." He flashed an impish grin and then swaggered down the hill.

Chapter Six
WONDERING

ON MY SECOND DAY ON THE ISLAND, Caleb invited me to walk with him along the beach. I soon suspected, though, from the determination in his quick and long strides, that our little walk was more than a healthful stroll; we seemed to be aiming toward something, going somewhere with a purpose, and following a time schedule. At first Caleb paid little mind to my slower gait, and whenever the distance between us grew more than the length of his shadow, I was forced to trot up beside him, where I enjoyed a few steps shoulder-to-shoulder with him before my small legs would again fall behind. After ten minutes of walking and running this way, Caleb finally turned back and noticed I was a bit winded. He reached out his hand, tousled my head, and then asked, "How'd you like a piggy-back ride, kid?" Then he squatted, placed his hands behind him, and told me to jump on. I did as he asked, and, as if I were a bag of goose feathers, he effortlessly lifted me onto his square, muscular back. Bobbing along with each step, my head to the right of his head, I was thrilled to see what it was like to be his height, to walk like Caleb, to be a Marine from the future.

I looked back on occasion to make note of the distance we had traveled, marking the beginning of our journey as the spot where two sets of footprints attenuated to one. But soon Caleb began to huff and puff, and the combination of tropical sun and the physical burden he carried on his back caused him to perspire—drops of sweat formed on the tip of his nose and his chin and then fell to the sand.

"All right, kiddo," he said, putting me down, a little out of breath. "We've reached our stop."

"Our stop?" I asked.

He looked down at me and smiled kindly. "Our destination," he clarified, and then pointed away from the sea toward a towering collection of sea-worn boulders.

"I did not know we had a destination," I said, now walking over the crest of the sandy beach alongside Caleb, the murmuring surf advancing and retreating behind us. The immense gathering of granite blocks immediately awed me. Had they been moved by the sea during a raging storm and placed, hodge-podge, one upon another? Rising at least a hundred feet, I imagined that this is how it would appear if an Egyptian pyramid had been toppled by an act of God, and I told Caleb so.

"There are no gods on this god-forsaken island," he said, holding his hand like a visor above his eyes and staring up to the tippy-top of the rocky formation.

"What are you looking for, Caleb?" I asked.

"Certainly not gods," he said, and then he walked into the shade of this massive jumble of rocks. "Pull up a chair, Prescott." I moved into the shade and sat next to him upon a smooth rock plastered with dried seaweed. A mixture of rotting organisms and sulfur accosted my nose—sea smells that reminded me of months spent upon a ship.

Caleb reached into a side pocket in his unusual trousers and retrieved a green flask that he called a canteen—he unscrewed the cap, took a swig, and then offered it to me. "You thirsty?"

I accepted the canteen and sniffed its musty opening. "Water?" I asked.

"No, it's urine, Prescott. I like to drink my own urine," he said, frowning.

Not realizing his sarcasm, my eyes were seashells—my arm froze with the flask a few inches from my lips.

"Ha-ha!" Caleb laughed. "You kill me. Yes, it's water. We're alone on an island, Pres. What? Were you expecting a Coke?"

I hesitantly drank from the flask, relieved that it was water, and then smiled at his foolishness.

"Ah, a smile!" he said. "I knew there was a 200-year old smile somewhere in that 12-year-old face." He gave me a brotherly shove by banging his bulky shoulder into mine. "I mention a Coke and get a smile—interesting."

"Coke?" I asked, as I handed back the flask.

"Never mind, kiddo," Caleb said, obviously very amused by my confusion, because he continued to chuckle at my expense. He took a sip and then returned the canteen to his trouser pocket. "You're a trip, Pres."

"Uh, thanks," I said, unsure if being a trip was a good or bad thing to be, but nevertheless unwilling to apprise him of my ignorance on the subject.

We sat there, some time, quietly looking out at the surf's gentle comings and goings; in truth, I was nearly lulled to sleep by its sequent rolls and sizzles upon the sand. And, minutes later, my head tipping forward as I nearly fell into a doze, Caleb startled me with a most unusual notion.

"I've been wondering, Pres," Caleb began. "Do you think we could be dead? I mean, how else do you explain it?"

"Explain what?"

"This," Caleb said, waving his hand in front of him. "This island. This mess we're in."

"Mess?" I asked.

"Pres, it's not exactly Disneyland," he said, his eyes squinting behind his spectacles. "Not that I expect you to know what that is," he added under his breath.

"Dead? No," I said, hesitantly. "I think that death would feel different."

"Really?" said Caleb, a large smile on his face. "You've been dead before?"

"No, of course not, but . . ." I thought about how Doctor Beckett might approach the subject. He had taught me to think logically, to find a scientific grounding in all things. "If I were dead," I began tentatively, "I would have no need to rest, eat, breathe—all my senses would be numb, would they not?"

Caleb picked up a small branch and began drawing arbitrary lines with it in the sandy soil. "I hear you," he said. "But I don't think that proves anything. Who's to say that death isn't like life? Maybe things continue on in death as they do in life? I mean . . . I don't know?" Caleb quickly snapped the stick in half and threw away the pieces.

"Before you came here, had you ever meet a man from 1968 before?"

"No," I acknowledged.

"That's because in life we don't suddenly meet and interact with people from another time. But here, on this island, we do."

"That makes us dead?"

"You have a better idea?"

"No—it all makes little sense," I said. "Yesterday I was aboard the *Bonhomme Richard*, north of England, and today I am near the equator with a man who was born 200 years after my birth."

Caleb revealed his brilliant white teeth. He was 17 years old, but appeared much younger, as if the men of the future required more years to mature. There was a youthful spirit in him that was unmistakably synonymous with adolescents in my time. He had more in common with someone my own age than he did with an adult. His mind, though, was strong, his reasoning sound, and his physical strength far superior to my own. I, after all, was half his weight.

"Right, Pres. It's not as if I've ever walked into a room in New England and an hour later found myself in Africa talking with some guy who was older than the U.S. Constitution. But in our case, it's crazy but true. I was in Vietnam a month ago, and now I'm a nowhere man in this nowhere land with some kid whose idea of modern warfare is a musket with a bayonet sticking out of it." Caleb half grunted, half laughed. "What else can it be, Pres? What is happening to us doesn't happen in life, in natural life."

"You are scaring me a little, Caleb?" I said, ashamed.

"You're not the only one scared, kid." Caleb took off his spectacles, blew away dust from the lenses, and put them back on.

"Is there no other explanation?" I said, tears suddenly welling in my eyes .

"None that I see," said Caleb, now standing and stretching his long arms.

A solitary tear coursed down my cheek. Caleb was so convincing, he was more experienced than me, and I admired him. But I still kept searching for some bit of reasoning that he had neglected. Then it suddenly arrived. "Caleb, maybe time is going backwards." I stood up, feeling empowered by the thought, and waited for his response.

"An interesting thought, Pres," Caleb said, walking away from me, poking his head into each dark space he found in the rocks, seemingly looking for something. "Now that I think about it," Caleb said, now shimmying sideways into another dark crevice in the rocks, "it would make much more sense to state that time is going backward rather than forward. I mean, it would explain why you arrived here after me."

"Then we are alive," I said.

Caleb, looking as though he were being consumed by the darkness between the rocks, revealed only his head. His smug expression—head tilted back, tight lips, eyes half-closed, and his head oscillating—told me he did not approve or subscribe to my newfound optimism. "We're not moving backward in time, or forward, or sideways, Pres. This island would give a clock a heart attack."

"Give a clock a . . . what are you talking about?" I could feel the tears welling again in my eyes. "I do not understand: is there time or is there no time?" I shouted this last statement, not because I was angry, but because Caleb's head popped down like a puppet into the darkness, into a shadowy fissure in the granite.

Then, like a jack-in-the-box, Caleb popped his head out and smiled curiously.

"You want to see something really wild, Pres?"

"What—an animal?"

"An animal? No, something really cool," he said, pointing into the dark space. "In here."

"It is cool in there?" I said.

"Pres!" Caleb, clearly annoyed by me, began moving his hands in front of his face like some addled person. "Would na-you," he said very slowly and in a speech pattern similar to a deaf person, "nike da see some-phin vew-wy int-er-mesting?"

"Why are you talking . . ."

He threw his head back in exasperation and then disappeared again into the dark space.

"Caleb?" I said, calling after him. "Wait for me!"

Chapter Seven
FINDING

MY SMALL SIZE MADE PASSING through the tight rocky space a much easier task than it was for Caleb, and two steps in I found myself submerged in a deathly darkness—the inside of a horse can be no darker. I held on to the scummy wall for balance and guidance, and felt my way with my feet, one small step, then another. The closed air inside the cave was especially pungent with smells of decomposition, which I optimistically attributed to the imagined moldering sea matter strewn around me, and fervently hoped that it was not a body—human or otherwise—putrid, sandy, maggot-infested, and wearing that grimace, that terror-filled and surprised mask that I have learned to associate with sudden fatality.

Up ahead, I heard the sound of shuffling shoes scrabbling among the stones. Then, as my eyes adjusted to the darkness, I saw Caleb, who cut a simian silhouette, hunched over and bobbing rhythmically.

"Caleb?" I said in a voice somewhat softer than I intended. "Is that you?"

"It's not Santa Claus," he said. There never seemed a time when his sense of humor deserted him. "But I do feel like I'm going up a chimney."

Several more steps and my feet met with knee-high rocks, which I tried to step over by lifting my right leg above them, but I only encountered more rocks, higher still.

"You'll have to do a little climbing," Caleb said, and I could clearly tell that his voice now came from above me.

Climbing ape-like—hand over foot—at an angle that exceeded sixty degrees at first, but got steeper still the farther up I clambered, I managed to gain on Caleb, and then could hear his heavy breathing and the rustle of his garments as he moved. Soon a faint radiance fell upon us, attaching itself like lichen to the irregular walls crowding in, chimney-like, around us. It was a strenuous activity to be climbing through this shaft, but I was eager to gain more elevation now that I realized the reward was sunlight.

Caleb loosened a stone the size of a cannon ball that barked my shins before it tumbled noisily past me.

"Are you hurt?" Caleb called down, after loosening the stone. I stopped to rub the pain out of my leg, and watched as Caleb moved steadily upward and out of view to the right. It was then that I realized that this shaft was twisting upwards like a corkscrew.

"I will live," I said, still rubbing the heartbeat out of my shin, before taking a deep breath and renewing the ascent.

When I finally emerged into bright sunlight, Caleb stood before me, sweat beading and running down his face and arms. He reached down and, with a formidable grip, nearly enveloped my hand in his large veined hand, then pulled me out of the rocky hole with the ease one would have lifting a kitten from a box, and then he gently placed me on my feet next to him.

"This is what I wanted to show you," he said, sweeping his right arm as he moved to the side of me.

Sunshine poured in—early morning light, whitish-yellow beams on a slant, making all appear alabaster. I sneezed.

"Bless you," said Caleb, patting me gently on the shoulder.

I did not respond to his blessing. I stood there, mouth agape, allowing my eyes and mind to adjust to my new surroundings. You have to remember that I had just emerged from a dark twisting shaft, and had expected to find myself at the top of the great mound of rocks, looking out at the sea. Instead, I stood in a twenty-foot by ten-foot chamber, furnished with a makeshift table, chairs, and bed, with walls and floor as smooth as glass and covered in the most unusual writing. I looked up and recognized remnants of a manmade roof—several small wooden poles still spanned the ten-foot opening, poles that I imagined once carried material, shingling perhaps, to keep out the weather. This roofing, though, had been gone a very long time, if the rotting wooden beams were a true indicator of its age. Scattered on the floor throughout the room were objects, some known to me, others complete mysteries.

"What is this place?" I finally asked, now stepping further into the chamber and knocking my knuckles on the round wooden table, which was cracked and faded by the sun and weather.

"It's Giovanni's home, and Ian's, and, of course, Christina's home," said Caleb, pointing right, then left, then down at the corner near me. "I bet Christina was a real beauty—soft hair pulled up in a loose bun, big eyes, and big . . ."

"What are you speaking about?"

"You can read, can't you?" Caleb said, that smug smile on his face. "Read for yourself." Caleb then squatted down and pointed toward the wall. There I read the name Christina O'Boyle, followed by numbers, presumably a date: "1975." I then scanned the room and began reading all the writing, which Caleb explained that the people of his time referred to as graffiti.

Above the bed scratched in loopy handwriting was written "Lawrence Connell," and the date "2006" next to it. On another wall, I read, "Dean Glines/Arrived here suddenly from Wales—1523." And a Sir Giovanni Morant, in black ink, simply scrawled next to his name, "It's hopeless!"

"Just how many souls shared this place?" I asked.

"It's impossible to tell, Pres," said Caleb, no longer squatting. "Think about it: if you and I were to write our names on the wall and the date we arrived here, it would be hundreds of years apart, and yet, here we are."

"Where are these people now?" I said, carefully sitting on the chair next to the table. It was crudely constructed and held together with a twine made from vinery. I was careful to set my legs securely on the floor before placing all of my weight on the chair, just in case it did not support my hundred pounds.

"I found this place three weeks ago," Caleb said, walking toward the far wall, near the bed of palm leaves. "This is my third visit," he continued, as he pushed aside some of the palm leaf bedding with the toe of his big black boot, "and every time I come here, I find something new." He suddenly bent over and reached behind the palm leaves. "Like this!"

Caleb pulled out an ivory colored object that I recognized as a ruff, an outdated piece of neck ornamentation worn by kings and queens that lived hundreds of years before me.

"It looks like an air filter for a car," said Caleb. "Do you know what it is?"

"Yes," I said, now standing and taking the object from Caleb. "You wear it around your neck." I placed the ruff around Caleb's bulging neck, but it was too small, so I put it around my neck.

"You look like an idiot," said Caleb, laughing. "It's like your head is sitting on a plate."

I took off the ruff and examined it. It was finely made, with not a blemish on it. It looked as though it were sewn yesterday.

Caleb reached behind the bedding again and pulled out another object. "Huh?" he said.

"What?"

"This wasn't here last time." He showed me a small, rectangular object made of a material that looked metallic, but was not. "You ever see one of these?" He then pulled on the object and it opened at one end, extending its length two times, but remaining open at an angle a little less than 180 degrees.

"I have never seen anything of the sort," I acknowledged.

Then Caleb did a strange thing. He placed the object against the side of his head, near his ear and along his jaw line. "Man, this is like something out of Star Trek. I know what this is," he said, amazed.

"What?"

"It's a communicator—a telephone," he said, a big smile on his face. He then spent several minutes explaining, or rather, trying to explain the concept of telephones to me. "This is not a telephone from my time, though. It's definitely from the future—the distant future. But the thing is dead," he said, pushing buttons on the belly-side of it. "It's hopeless." This last statement eerily echoed the sentiments scrawled on the wall by Sir Giovanni.

Caleb heaved the phone with great strength over the walls and out of the chamber.

"Is there anything else there?" I asked, pointing toward the bedding.

"Nothing new," he said, now bending over and fishing through the bedding. "Wait! What is this?" He withdrew a piece of paper that had been carefully folded several times. After unfolding the paper, he pulled it closer to his eyes and studied it. "Prescott?"

"Yes?"

"I don't suppose you read French, do you?"

"I do not."

Caleb seemed disappointed. "Neither do I," he admitted, and then folded the paper and placed it in his trouser pocket.

Caleb moved over and sat upon the chair I recently vacated. He looked up at the sky and mumbled, "Another perfect day in paradise."

I kicked at the palm leaf bedding, but did not reveal any new objects of interest. Then I took the seat across from Caleb and placed my hands on the table. I looked up at the sky and noticed that the sun was nearly directly above us. There was not a cloud in the sky. I looked over at Caleb. He was now leaning back and seemingly studying his great big boots, but I could tell he was lost in thought, and his knitted eyebrows concerned me.

"Caleb," I began, hesitantly. "Why did you bring me here?"

Caleb broke from his trance and smiled sheepishly. "I don't know."

"I do not know what to make of it either," I said. "Look at all these names, all these dates. How can it be?"

"This island," said Caleb. "It's a mystery. I've been here for a month and, believe me, what I concluded is that it's a mystery, Prescott. It's a lousy mystery."

"I do not like this mystery," I said, tears forming in my eyes.

"Hey, kiddo," Caleb said, getting up. "Don't let it get you down."

"How can I help it?"

"Pres, how would you like a reverse history lesson?"

"A what? Reverse history?"

"How would you like to know how it all turns out? You know, the future," Caleb said excitedly. "It'll be story time—a traveling story. Except, I'll tell you about the future."

"Traveling story?" I said, getting up. "Where are we traveling to?"

"Back to the hooch—our home above the cliffs," said Caleb, putting his arm around my back.

And Caleb was good to his word. Caleb told me fascinating information about machines and battles and countries that I had never before heard tell of. He enjoyed speaking of weapons of war, fantastic bombs that eliminate cities, and firearms that shoot repeatedly, accurately, and at great distances.

"Will you tell me about the machines of medicine?" I asked later that night, as the fire smoldered and decreased in brightness, and I now lay in bed.

"I'll tell you everything you want to know, man. We've got all the time in the world, right?"

"I do not know? Do we?" I said, feeling like crying again.

I learned of drugs that put people to sleep and feel no pain, I learned of doctors opening up a patient's chest and fixing the heart, and I learned of incredible machines that measure every heartbeat.

Increasing lengths of silence crept between our conversations, and Caleb had the last word that night.

As my heavy eyelids covered my eyes, I heard him say, in that unusual accent, the following words, "Prescott, I've had no one to talk with for a month—or what feels like a month. Tonight I'm not alone. Whether I'm dead or alive, or somewhere in the middle, it doesn't matter, because I can tell you one thing that is darn well true: I'm glad that you're here and I'm not alone anymore."

Chapter Eight
PROVISIONING

ONCE WE BROACHED AND ACCEPTED as fact the issue of our apparent time travel; and once we understood that a fascinating, nearly unfathomable, and extremely unsettling life change had been predicated upon us, the gulf of the two centuries that divided us rapidly closed in, and nearly all of our differences were nullified, though there were occasional inconveniences regarding communication.

The next morning while in my palm-lead bed in Caleb's hooch, I soon realized that people from my time period were better prepared for what Caleb termed "camping out." Caleb had made many errors in judgment regarding the placement of his hooch and the material he used to construct it. Over the next week, I would aid him in placing the hooch between two large boulders, which served as natural barriers to the trade winds and would shelter us from greater winds during tropical storms. Caleb had harnessed the use of fire, but he was greatly aware that his cigarette lighter would eventually run out of lighter fluid. I showed him how to properly bank the fire so he could reuse the coals the next day to rekindle a new fire, thereby eliminating the need to use his lighter at all. We both agreed that he should conserve the lighter, a remarkable invention that was obviously the grandchild notion of the flint and steel method commonly used in my time.

Caleb tried catching fish using the poles that I had seen standing upright in the sand when I arrived on the island. He angled for fish by attaching sinew to a pole, fashioning a razor-sharp hook out of shell casings of a few spent bullets, and using his dog tags (those metallic plates that had attracted my attention on my first day) as shiny lures. This method failed, however, so he placed shell casings over the tips of the poles and began successfully spearing the abundant white bass.

Food was plentiful on the island. There were coconuts, kiwi—and other tropical fruits—and much small game (rats, mice, squid, and snakes). A particular squat, plump, and flightless genus of bird, with a hooked beak and unintelligent eyes, waddled out of the thick jungle brush and onto the beach each evening. These noisy, dun-colored creatures would walk among us, fearful of nothing, apparently because they had no natural enemy on the island. Caleb and I would gather one of these animals by enveloping it in my waistcoat and, later, enjoy a rather delicious feast. And though we continued to slaughter this witless bird, the flock never changed its habit of visiting our beach, nor did it ever modify its behavior when near to us. Caleb called this animal a dodo bird, but I am nearly certain it is not the correct appellation for this species.

Caleb and I quickly developed a successful routine for survival on the island. We also became fast friends, as our personalities, though starkly different, were suitable to each other. We talked constantly. We discussed philosophy, history—much of it the future to me—and developed new theories about the island and why we were mysteriously placed upon it.

A superficial understanding of science made it easy for me to make deductions about the island's weather patterns. This was not New England by any stretch of the imagination, and therefore not as difficult to forecast the day's weather.

I knew that one can predict the weather fairly accurately by studying the sky—more precisely, by studying the clouds. Doctor Beckett taught me advanced science and I, a greedy student, begged him each day to teach me more.

As a sailor, or an apprentice to a sailing doctor, I was familiar with the saying, "Red skies at night, sailor's delight; red skies in the morning, sailors take warning." Grounded in this adage was good science.

Using this basic method of forecasting, I knew it would be simple to predict when a storm might arrive. In addition, I noticed a daily pattern in the island weather. There were cool trade winds at dawn, then a steady increase in the air temperature and humidity. As the sun rose in the sky, there were occasional sun-showers of a minute's duration. The rain usually evaporated within a quarter of an hour, as more tropical sun beamed down upon the island. Then showers of greater length occurred in the early evening.

Science taught me that the sun drove the weather cycle. The sun's energy evaporated the water, the trees and vegetation transpired, and the moisture climbed to the heavens as the heated air rose. After a daylong collection of moisture, great cumulonimbus clouds formed and, unable to carry the weight of the millions of water particles, fell to the earth in the form of rain.

I explained my theories to Caleb one morning as we collected bananas and coconuts from trees along the edge of the beach. I did not think it likely that he knew of this science, but he did.

Caleb interrupted my lecture on weather, smiled smugly, and then patted me on the back. "No offense, Prescott, but that is grade school information in the 20th century."

The more I learned about the future, the more I tended to feel inferior, which no doubt I was; however, I reminded myself—and occasionally Caleb—that the future was built upon the shoulders of the people in the past, and therefore I and my colonial contemporaries were instrumental in leading toward all the wondrous advances in the future. Furthermore, I made it a habit to remind myself that the future was a part of me, and I a part of the future. It is impossible, after all, to separate the wood from the tree.

By virtue of my young age, small stature, inexperience in the world, and lack of general knowledge, especially my ignorance of all inventions and other such cleverness that evolved in the ages that followed my own, I should have felt as a subordinate or an underling to Caleb. It was not so, however, because Caleb treated me as his equal, often deferring to me about what to do next with our time. I began to believe that the men of the future did not equate age with status the way it was during my time, a time that Caleb termed Colonial Times. I remember feeling bigger than my breeches as Caleb continually asked for my opinion on matters and then showed me that he valued my thoughts. Furthermore, Caleb was quick to compliment me on a job well done or something well learned, and he readily gave consideration to my suggestions, even when his experience told him they were naïve or even silly.

One of my first suggestions was about acquiring a second home. I believed that we should continue to maintain the perch above the seaside cliffs, but should have another dwelling away from the open air. A cave, I suggested, would be preferred over building a wooden structure with a roof, which is what Caleb suggested. Neither one of us had any carpentry skills, nor did we possess any building tools.

"We should search the interior of the island for a cave," I said, as we stood ankle deep in the seawater one late afternoon. "Out there, beyond the whorled vines is a well-worn path that may lead us to civilization, an abandoned house, or a cave that we can go to when— or if—a tropical storm arrives."

For some reason, Caleb resisted my suggestion to walk inland, and he was especially averse to exploring that trail. That said, Caleb did not express his distaste with my plan, he was much too well mannered and polite to do that, but his sagging shoulders, the pained expression on his face, and his clenched fists provided all the visual clues that I required.

"We do not have to go now," I said, talking to the back of his head. He held a steel-tipped pole in his hand now and tracked the movement of a sea bass swimming through the shallow teal seawater. Caleb then flicked his powerful wrist, sending the pole into the water, and then lifted the pole to reveal a speared white bass.

"It's safe out here," Caleb said, pulling the wriggling fish off of the spear. "We have all the food we want to eat. It's comfortable, right? So why leave?"

"I do not want to leave," I said, holding out the green canvas bag that Caleb called his rucksack. Caleb dropped the fish into the bag. "I believe we should provision—prepare for a time when the weather could become dangerous. I recall a time when . . ."

Caleb and I began walking toward the sandy beach. "You may find that a hurricane is less dangerous than what you will find in there," interrupted Caleb, indicating the path behind the vines by thrusting out his chin in that direction.

"Caleb," I said, stopping in my tracks, the surf splashing at my ankles. "Have you been in there? Have you walked along the hard-packed trail?"

"I've been in there," he said, quietly, now peering powerfully into my eyes. "As a matter of fact, that is where I came from."

Chapter Nine
PRATTLING

DURING MY SECOND DAY ON THE ISLAND, Caleb heated fresh water in a green metallic container that I later learned doubled as a battle helmet. The ingenuity of the future fascinated me then—as it does now.

As the water boiled, Caleb recalled a time during his first week on the island when, walking along the edge of the jungle, he discovered a vast growth of cacao plants thriving in the shade of the massive canopied trees. He gathered these light brown pods, or beans, and then spread them out in the sun. When dried, Caleb pulverized the beans with a tomato-sized stone, and then placed the brown powder into hot water, thus producing what he called hot cocoa. Caleb explained to me that, though the drink was not as sweet as he liked it, it was still better than drinking unflavored hot water. Though not up to snuff, Caleb proclaimed the drink much better than any other concoctions he made using leaves and berries found on the island.

"I made the mistake, when I first got here, of drinking about 16 ounces of a minted drink that I made by dropping an oval-shaped, dark green leaf into my boiling water. The taste was far-out; the after-result was horrible—I threw up the entire contents of my stomach, including the first dodo bird that I ate."

"How do you know that it was not the bird that made you ill?" I wondered, making conversation.

"Prescott, did you barf after you ate a dodo?"

"Barf?"

"Vomit," explained Caleb, and then smiled at my confusion. He seemed to relish every time a modern idiom confused me. I found, as I grew to know him more, and as I began to increase my knowledge of the modern idioms, that he would search for obscure words just to spite me; and I do not doubt that he coined a few words of his own and passed them off as being "absolutely legitimate." The fact is that things clearly within view, Caleb would term "out of sight." Abstract things—concepts and memories—that are impalpable, and therefore always out of sight in the most literal sense, Caleb also termed "out of sight." I quickly understood that this unusual and nonsensical idiom was used to describe a thing, feeling, or thought that is wonderful, brilliant, or unusual.

I sometimes used idiomatic phrases that I thought would confuse Caleb, but they rarely did; they all seemed familiar to him, which I found to be a comfort, because it meant that my contemporaries, now all dusty bones in cold crypts beneath the ground, are, in a very tenuous way, a part of the future, and therefore a particle of immortality. The future builds itself on the framework of the past.

As we sat by the fire sipping cocoa and watching a meteor shower blossom above the central volcanic peak of the island, I explained to Caleb that if I ever returned to the *Bonhomme Richard*, Admiral Jones would "flip his wig." What I figured would be a perplexing statement Caleb comprehended easily.

"Yeah," Caleb said. "Sergeant McGuire will flip his wig if I ever get back to Da Nang—especially because I've been A.W.O.L thirty-something days."

"A.W.O.L?" He had done it again. I was confused by the future.

"A.W.O.L. is an acronym that stands for A—absent, W—with, O—out, L—leave. Sergeant McGuire never gave me permission to leave. I'd sooner be able to kiss my own elbows before I'd convince the Sarge that I spent thirty days on a desert island alone, until a Colonial kid paid me a visit."

I sipped the hot cocoa and acknowledged my understanding with a nod of the head.

"If I told Sarge about you and this island, he'd send me to a rubber room, where some shrink would make me read ink blots." Caleb picked up a small shell and flung it over the cliff. Then, after reading the confusion in my face, he smiled satisfactorily. "In my time, they put the mentally insane who are believed to be a danger to themselves in a padded cell, which is referred to as a rubber room; and we call a psychiatrist a 'shrink,' because, figuratively-speaking, it shrinks your head by reducing tension."

I tried to mask my confusion by nodding my head to show understanding, but I know I did not fool him. Eager to meet Caleb on level ground, I returned to our former discussion. "How do you know that you did not eat a diseased dodo bird? That mint-flavored leaf may be perfectly safe to drink in hot water. You could be . . . "

"I repeat, Prescott, dodos do NOT upset my stomach. I've eaten about twenty of them and never felt sick, never vomited."

Reason told me to agree with Caleb, but something inside of my psyche (call it pride intermingled with an eagerness to regain some of the intellectual ground that I had lost as a result of being in the dark about 200 years of linguistic history), caused me to question and play the devil's attorney.

"Suppose," I began, "that you contracted a flu of the stomach? That could make you vomit, could it not?"

"Yes, Dr. Prescott . . ."

"Fielding."

"What?"

"My surname is Fielding—but I'm not a doctor; I'm a doctor's apprentice."

"Yes, Dr. Fielding—it could," said Caleb in a very childish monotone.

"A true scientist leaves nothing to chance," I continued. "Variables abound in the scenarios that you have produced for me." I thought at that time about how proud Doctor Beckett would have been of that statement, which was something I had heard the good doctor say on many occasions, especially when a patient began providing his own diagnosis.

I stood up, crossed my arms, and leaned against the large boulder. The meteor shower continued, streak after ephemeral streak, dashing and dying along the horizon.

"Your indigestion and upset stomach, Caleb, could have been caused by a piece of rank fish that you ate for lunch, or from ingesting a tiny bit of a poisonous resin from one of the many plants that you touched that day. The resin could have easily been transferred from your hand to your mouth, because I have noticed that you bite your nails, and often you have your hands in your mouth."

"Prescott," said Caleb, in an even tone.

"Yes?"

"It was the minted leaf."

"How can you be sure?" I inquired, laughing a little.

"I'm sure."

"Well, you know . . ."

"Prescott, I'm sure."

I muttered some more thoughts on the subject under my breath and then retreated to my bed for a night's repose.

The next evening, Caleb announced that he had concocted a drink and named it in my honor.

"Drink up. I think you'll find that this drink, this drink I call Prescott Fielding, is very satisfying."

He had flavored the hot water with a spicy mint. It was delicious. After I downed the entire contents of the metallic cup, I proclaimed pompously that a shipment of those leaves into New England would capsize the tea industry. This made Caleb very happy.

Less than an hour later, I vomited my insides out.

"Do you still think it's the dodo?" I heard Caleb say, as I bent over and wiped the spittle from my lips.

I stood up straight, turned to him and announced, "I suppose that Prescott Fielding is unpalatable no matter how you take it—in a hot mug or via a lecture on variables."

Caleb got a great laugh from this statement, patted me on the back, and told me I was "the cat's pajamas."

I lay down on my bed and contemplated this latest cryptic statement, my stomach still churning.

"And you, Caleb—Caleb, you're something that includes a dog, some clothing, and something witty—the point of which I am too tired to extricate from this pudding head of mine . . . I suppose it's my just dessert."

Chapter Ten
REFLECTING

THAT EVENING, as a bank of cumulus clouds played at changing colors along the horizon—from orange to lavender to pink—and the disappearing day reluctantly spirited off to hide behind the moon, Caleb asked me about my pre-island life. He explained that what he knew of my time was gleaned from the pages of history books.

"Give it to me straight," he said, sitting across from me, his long legs stretched out and crossed at the ankles. "What was it like in 1770s?"

What follows is a condensed version of what I told Caleb across the campfire.

I was born into an aristocratic English family in Norwich, a town in the Colony of Connecticut, in 1766, and then sent across the Atlantic to be schooled in London until just before my tenth birthday. It was 1776 and the thirteen colonies were revolting against England, so my parents sent for me to return home. I sailed into Rhode Island Colony in late June of that year, during the time that John Adams and Thomas Jefferson were in Philadelphia putting the final flourishes on the Declaration of Independence. I then traveled northwest by coach to Providence, where my parents were renting a small home that my father termed a "transition house." Within a fortnight of my arrival all of our belongings were packed into several wagons and towed north, to the great city of Boston. Politically speaking, things were not settled in Boston at this time. General Washington and his ragtag army would soon surround the city and, by wielding the power of their newly mounted cannons, convince the British Army and about a thousand Loyalists to board ships docked in Boston Harbor and then sail north to Canada.

My father, an indefatigable Patriot, was an attorney-at-law. He plied his trade by day in the small front room of our Beacon Hill home, and by night he attended boisterous but secretive meetings in the attics of what he termed his "brothers," but whom I knew were none other than the infamous Sons of Liberty.

My relationship with my father was estranged, no doubt because I had been away from home for more than four years. I fulfilled the primary duty that every son must—to honor and obey his mother and father; yet, I felt alien in my own home. My father provided the basic needs and, because he was a wealthy man, many creature comforts too. For instance, I had my own mare and my own bedchamber furnished with a handsome featherbed, a looking glass, and a mahogany washstand with silver hardware.

The imminent civil war between England and her American colonies greatly abridged my formal education; nevertheless, my father deemed my intellect and character to be fit for success in the field of medicine, so in a matter of days I was living a stone's throw from the North Church, where I began my doomed apprenticeship under Doctor Marlowe Shepard at his Charter Street home, across from the Copps Hill Cemetery, that final resting place for Boston's original population.

Doctor Shepherd was an old codger with distaste for true science and a proclivity for pouring ale into his distended gullet. I spent only seven weeks under Dr. Shepherd, but learned a great deal in that time because I did much of the work. It was a trial by fire, as Dr. Shepherd was rarely sober enough to tend to his patients, a responsibility that fell upon me. Inexperienced though I was, I did manage well enough, until a prominent citizen, Ezekiel Pearth, entered with what he termed a brain fever. Doctor Shepard instructed me to bleed Mr. Pearth, and I dutifully did so, but nearly to the point of death; I could not get the wound to congeal. Panicked, the ashen-faced Mr. Pearth demanded that Doctor Shepard personally tend to his wound and immediately "put a stop to this amateurish letting." Doctor Shepard then stumbled into the room, all too in his cups—he could not hold his own head up more than a few seconds at a time, and was therefore useless to Mr. Pearth. The poor patient, his face the color of snow, tied a tourniquet around the wound and removed himself from the building immediately.

Mr. Pearth visited my father the very next day, and that evening my father informed me that my apprenticeship with Dr. Shepherd was over. "I shall find a proper physician for your apprenticeship," my father promised. "Even if it must be Nathaniel Beckett."

Beckett it was. Renowned for his skills as a physician and surgeon, Dr. Beckett was a controversial figure in Boston. Many citizens, including my own father, suspected Dr. Beckett of being a Loyalist, while holding in high regard his knowledge of anatomy and medicine.

Within a fortnight of my new placement, my parents were dead, burned to death in their Beacon Hill home. My mother, as I later learned, had stoked the fire before turning in that evening, and an ember jumped onto her dress, began burning madly, and then enveloped her in flames. My father, hearing her blood-curdling screams, leapt onto her in an attempt to smother the fire, but this only added more fuel to the blaze, as my father's clothes ignited too. My mother died in my father's arms, and from this I gain comfort. It took twelve hours longer for my father's suffering to end. He had dragged himself into the street, where a passerby found him gasping for breath. He was immediately carried to the house of Doctor Beckett, burnt beyond recognition; I had to be told of his identity. That evening his breathing grew shallower and shallower. I held his charred hand until mortal strength and spirit simultaneously left him.

My father's will and testament indicated that all of his worldly possessions were to be given to my much older brother, my only sibling. It was stipulated that I was to receive a little more than one-third the proceeds from the sale of my father's estate and fifty percent of his liquid assets when I finished my apprenticeship, some time in my seventeenth year.

A strange thing it is to bury your parents. I felt as though my heart was made of the same material as the shovel that threw the loose dirt onto their coffins. Dry-eyed and cloud-headed, I was led away by Doctor Beckett, who guided me gently by the wrist to his house.

The tears continually coursed down my cheeks that night and the next as the weather mirrored my own feelings, until on the third day, the Sabbath, the thunderclouds opened to reveal the hidden sun, and the twitter of birds replaced the sound of the pattering rain.

It did not take long to settle back into my position as a physician's apprentice. I began curing, bleeding, and comforting patients, under the direct supervision of my master, a kindly master, a man who, with no children of his own, treated me as a son from the very beginning—more so after my parents' tragic deaths. I greatly missed my parents, but Doctor Beckett's attentions and kindness made the transition out of mourning a much easier process.

In the three months that we spent in Boston, I assisted Doctor Beckett as he performed two memorable operations.

Tucker Wilson, the sturdy 12-year-old son of a local silversmith, fell from a tree and fractured his shin in several places. The only viable option was to amputate the leg just below the knee, which Doctor Beckett carried out using a tool that resembled a woodsman's saw. I carried the limb out behind the house, and under the doctor's orders, consigned it to flames. This was a particularly difficult task, especially when you consider that as I watched the skin curl and char, I naturally thought about my parents' horrible end—I cringed at the thought of flames rendering my mother's beautiful face into something shapeless and hideous.

Tucker survived the amputation, but was not a productive member of the community thereafter. Doctor Beckett had correctly predicted that Tucker's future would be as a charity case at the almshouse.

Late in the summer of 1776 the grandsons of William Thacker carried him into Doctor Beckett's house, bleeding profusely from a shoulder wound. Thacker's youngest grandson, Jacob, had accidentally discharged his musket and shot him. The musket ball was lodged deep in the shoulder, near the trapeze muscle. The good doctor had me poke around the oozing shoulder for nearly a half hour in an attempt to extricate the ball while he, using all of his might and weight, manhandled the patient to keep him still, all the while enduring the ghoulish screams and the wriggling of the patient's tortured body. When I removed the ball, my master quickly sewed and bandaged the wound, and then released him to the care of his adult niece. Thacker returned a week later to present my master with a two-year old mare.

My father's assumption was incorrect about my new master; Doctor Beckett was not loyal to the crown. But I should temper that remark by stating that, during those first few months after the colonies declared independency from the mother country—when the world seemed to turn upside down—Doctor Beckett remained neutral.

Around this time, Doctor Beckett introduced me to Revered Clay Winthrop, an important Bostonian and a great Patriot. Over the course of two days, the reverend and my master had what Doctor Beckett termed, "Many life-changing conversations."

These conversations were instrumental in convincing Doctor Beckett to apply his surgical skills in the war effort. I remember one night when Reverend Winthrop asked my master how his sea legs were. The good doctor said it was well past his time to develop the sea legs necessary to become a surgeon aboard a battleship. The reverend rose and calmly said, "Time means nothing," a statement that now drips with irony, considering our present circumstances on this island.

Reverend Winthrop brushed his hand across the white pew door, and then said, "Go back to your practice, Nathaniel. I'll write to you on occasion, and, if the political problems persist, I may call on you."

I knew of Reverend Winthrop's association with Samuel Adams, Paul Revere, and several of the other infamous Patriots; therefore, I knew the serious implications in this statement.

Three years later, after much correspondence with Reverend Winthrop, now living in Philadelphia, Doctor Beckett and I traveled to France, and soon after joined the crew of the *Bonhomme Richard*.

Chapter Eleven
INFERRING

AND WHO WAS CALEB THOMPSON?

To start with, he stood ten inches taller than me—more than six feet tall. His hair was clipped short, a little longer than stubble. He wore spectacles, heavy dark frames shaped like circles that had been crushed flat on the top. Clothed, his body appeared thin and lanky, but his shirtsleeves were always rolled up just below the shoulder, revealing arms that bulged with sinewy muscle and were capable of great leverage. He wore baggy trousers with pockets that ran down the sides. He called these trousers "fatigues." I imagined it would be fatiguing to walk around with all the things he carried in those pockets. Caleb carried a multitude of odd articles in his pockets; I am always amazed at how much he brought with him to this island. One evening, as we sat by the fire, reposing after a hard day's work, Caleb emptied his pockets and displayed all that he carried from that other life—a story for another time.

The skin on Caleb's cheeks, upper lip, and chin, was whiskerless. Because of his young countenance, it was easy for me to think of him as a boy. However, when Caleb stripped down to only his undergarments (he called them his underwear), as he did whenever he went for a swim in the sea, Caleb looked like a man. His shoulders were broad and packed with muscle. His hairless chest was chiseled—each pectoral muscle greatly defined. His flat stomach also rippled with muscle, and his quadriceps must have been 25 inches in diameter—all that power lay hidden under baggy fatigues.

"Are all the men of the future as fit as you?"

"Naw," he said. "Most of the men in the Marines—yes—but not the typical man."

"Remarkable," I said. "So what is the typical man like?"

Caleb's eyes narrowed.

"I don't know, Prescott," he said, somewhat bemused and slightly embarrassed. "I guess . . ." He blew air through his pursed lips. "They're kind of fat and out of shape."

"You guess?" I said, half seriously. "You mean you do not truly know?" I paused for comedic timing. "Perhaps you need new spectacles."

Caleb laughed. The merriment was contagious, and for reasons I still do not understand, we both began cackling like two drunkards on our way out of a tavern.

I was interested in Caleb, and wanted to learn more about him and his past. But Caleb was rarely forthcoming with information when it involved himself. When, one night, two weeks after my arrival on the island, I pressed Caleb for more information about his pre-island existence, he was evasive and ambiguous.

"Let's just say, Prescott," began Caleb, as he bit into the leg of a boiled dodo, "where I am now is a huge improvement over where I was."

Chapter Twelve
RAGING

LIGHTNING DISCHARGED ANGRILY IN THE DARK DISTANCE, illuminating for only a heartbeat the spectral shapes of the silent clouds. The surf pounded the shore below, while thunder, reverberating like cannon fire, boomed persistently from above. Great bullets of water sprayed down in the howling gusts of wind. Palm branches snapped, fell, and blew across our plateau in the frantic storm-driven vortex, while the green plastic tarpaulin used for the roof of the hooch whipped and snapped frantically until it finally flew away over the cliff.

The hooch roof now gone, Caleb and I were quickly soaked to the skin, our campfire extinguished, and our spirits dashed.

"We can't stay here," yelled Caleb over the noises of the storm. He pointed to the sky. "The lightning, the wind—it's too dangerous up here!"

Caleb hurriedly gathered his belongings and thrust them inside his rucksack; I gathered what I had brought—all of which fit into the pockets of my garments, and then we scurried toward the precipitous path that led to the beach below.

I slipped and fell twice, before reaching sea level. The second fall caused me to badly scrape my knee, tearing my canvas breeches in the process. Blood, thinned by the rainwater, coursed from my wound and discolored the front of my trousers below the knee.

The pelting rain continued, and bolts of lightning, with countless capillaries of electrical energy radiating from the main artery, produced deafening thunder that resonated in my chest and scared me half to death.

"Head for the trees!" Caleb yelled in my ear. "Quick!"

I ran behind Caleb, watching the lightning illuminate his shape, temporarily casting flickering shadows of form on the sand. Caleb's physical conditioning, as I have remarked before, was far superior to my own; therefore, it is no surprise that I soon fell well behind. My injured leg motivated me little to quicken my pace, although the increased potential for being a conductor of electricity encouraged me to increase my pace from a saunter to a slow jog.

Caleb moved past the stone statues holding skull and flower, and then disappeared behind the wildly rustling vines that divided the beach and the jungle.

When I pushed aside the vines, I found Caleb kneeling near the trunk of a colossal tree with broad serrated leaves.

"Prescott!" he called. "Come on in—the weather's fine."

Water dropped out of his closely cropped brown hair and down his face. Fog covered his spectacles, hiding his eyes. Caleb grinned widely. This weather pleased him. The excitement invigorated him. Perhaps, the tranquility of the island life we had come to expect was too tame for him, especially when you juxtapose the normally serene island life with what he considered his previous life on the battlefields of Vietnam.

I crouched and crawled under the branches and then sat next to Caleb. We both leaned perpendicular to each other against the same trunk.

"So," I began, trying to speak as I regained my normal breathing. The temperature on the island had dropped considerably, and I could see my breath as I spoke. "We have finally visited the path beyond the stone statues together."

Caleb grunted his acknowledgement of this fact.

We sat silently for some time and listened to the storm. Then the sound of the raindrops landing on the leaves above slowed.

"What if . . ." I started.

"Great," Caleb interrupted. "Dr. Fielding is getting behind the lectern again."

"What?" I said, and leaned forward a little to look at him.

Caleb had pulled out his shirttail and was rubbing the glass lenses of his spectacles clean. He then placed his spectacles on his face, turned to me, crossed his eyes, and drew his lips far back, revealing nearly every tooth in his mouth.

"No, I am not going to lecture you. I am merely going to suggest that we should take this opportunity to explore the path. Perhaps, we could . . ."

"No, Prescott," he interrupted.

"Hear me out," I said, raising my voice.

"Prescott, we've gone over this before. I'm not going back in there."

"Why? I cannot understand your fear?"

The ground began to tremble, softly at first, and then more violently. In a matter of seconds it was calm again.

"Huh," said Caleb. "Do you know what that was?"

"An earthquake."

"Yes," he said quietly. "Or the volcano is beginning to stir."

"If it erupts, do we stand a chance?"

"Not a chance."

We sat quietly again, anticipating more quaking of the earth. When it did not arrive, and the pattering of the rain on the leaves ceased completely, I used this new quiet to think and to finally gather the courage necessary to stand up, take a deep breath, and announce to Caleb, "I have decided that, with or without you, I am going to explore the path."

"Is that right, little man?" said Caleb, now rising to his feet.

"Of course, I would prefer you to go with me, especially because you have been inland before. But, if you will not, and must remain stubborn . . ."

"Stubborn, eh?" For some reason this made Caleb laugh.

"Yes, stubborn seems to be the correct word in this case."

"Is this a case?"

"Caleb, you know the meaning of my words."

"Oh, ease up, Pres."

"I would greatly appreciate any information about where the path leads so that I can prepare myself."

"It's a long story," Caleb said. "You're in too much of a rush."

I reached for Caleb's rucksack, placing it between the trunk of the tree and me, and then knelt down and leaned back on it. I folded my hands in front of my stomach, crossed my legs at the ankles, and said, "I have all the time in the world."

"We don't know what time is anymore." Caleb sat down next to me, deftly pulled his rucksack away from me, causing me to flop back against the rough bark of the tree, and then reclined against the rucksack.

I moved across from Caleb and sat cross-legged. When he did not speak, I said, "I'm waiting?"

"Where do I begin?"

"How about the beginning?" I said, and then pulled a funny face of my own.

"You mean Vietnam?"

"If it makes sense?"

"Nothing in Vietnam makes sense."

Chapter Thirteen
HEARING THE SUN

"VIETNAM, MAN—what's going on in Nam is not a popular thing," began Caleb, as he sat with me beneath that broad-leaved tropical tree. "Much of the United States hates it—hates the conflict, the war, whatever you want to call it. I heard that guys are going back home after fighting in Nam, after risking their lives, and instead of being heroes, they are treated like dirt—like murderers."

When Caleb turned 17 years old, the government drafted him for military service in the United States Army.

"There's a bunch of ways to avoid the draft," explained Caleb. "They won't make you go if you're still in school, or if you're an only-son, or if you have friends in high places who can use their power to keep your butt away from the battlefield, or . . . if you pack up your crap and head north to Canada."

Caleb asked for and was granted a transfer into the United States Marine Corps.

"I figured," said Caleb, explaining why he transferred, "that if I'm going to die, I might as well die wearing the best uniform. It was all about an image—stupid, really. To be honest, I pictured myself wearing the dress blue Marine uniform, with blood-red stripes shooting down the sides of my pant legs, marching in some Fourth of July parade while high school classmates looked on in admiration, classmates who maybe didn't respect me, or who thought I wasn't cool enough for their clique. I don't know. Looking back it's kind of dumb. It seems like a long time ago." Caleb patted me on the leg and laughed a little. "You want to know the funny thing? The funny thing is that I never got those dress blues. I got regulation green fatigues like all the other grunts that they send to Nam."

Caleb changed directions in his story.

"My parents divorced when I was thirteen," he said. "My dad moved to the West Coast—California—and I only saw him two more times before he died. My mom raised me. She didn't make much money, but she was always there for me. Always." A bead of perspiration slowly slid from Caleb's temple down his cheek. "My mom constantly cried the week before I left for Marine Corps basic training. I hated to see her cry, but there was a weird part of me that liked it. It made me feel like a man—I realize now that I was a jerk. I'd love to tell her how sorry . . . how much I love and miss her."

When Caleb stated that his recruiting officer put him on a train heading south, I interrupted to ask for clarification about the word "train." Caleb, patient as ever, told me about the various modes of modern transportation in his time. He spoke of airplanes, trains, automobiles, tanks, tractors, and many other versions of what he called internal combustion engines, before returning to his story.

"The train carried me from Boston to South Carolina, where I hopped on a bus with a bunch of other recruits and rode to Parris Island. That was the beginning of the end of my previous life.

"I don't want to die now and I didn't want to die then. So, I was scared. I didn't have anything against the Vietnamese. They didn't know me. I didn't know them. But here I was being trained to kill them. Why? Because if I didn't they would kill me. It's messed up."

Caleb landed in Vietnam on August 17, 1968.

"The air in Nam rots. The most humid day on this island is dry compared to Nam. And Nam smells like trash and crap and death—all mixed with an orange dust that blows everywhere, in everything—your mouth, eyes, nose, food.

"I was in the infantry," Caleb explained after a brief pause. "My platoon spent every day going on long walks, which the Marines call humping, in search of the enemy. It was the worst—scary. You never knew what was around the next bend, around the next corner. Nam's a jungle, and there's razor-sharp elephant grass that slices your skin when you touch it. And the bugs and rats . . ." Caleb shuddered to show his disgust.

"It was a simple plan. Our job was to find Charlie—code name for the Viet Cong. But some Marines got a little crazy, you know? War does that. When a landmine blows up your buddy and you don't know who planted it, well . . . it messes with your head. Some guys fought back the only way they could—by bullying the villagers, shooting their livestock, stealing their food and whatever else they wanted from the huts, slapping the kids around—it was kind of sick, screwed up."

Caleb pulled his legs in close and then hugged his knees. There was a sad faraway look in his eyes. He inhaled deeply, shook his head as if trying to dislodge something disagreeably clinging to him, and then exhaled. "Here's the funny thing—we didn't know who our enemy was. The Vietnamese barber on base who, by day, cuts your hair and shaves your beard with a straight razor, could be a Viet Cong sniper by night that's trying to shoot you. We didn't know—that was the toughest part."

On November 3, 1968, Caleb and his platoon humped toward Hill 19.

"I'd never seen combat in my two months in Nam. I knew, though, that it was happening all the time. I saw men—or what used to be men—jammed into body bags, loaded onto choppers every day. I'd seen the Viet Cong dead piled six feet high, their mouths open, flies buzzing in and out. That gruesome sight will stay with me forever—those dead men stripped of their clothing, missing ears (some Marines cut off Viet Cong ears to keep as souvenirs). The dead looked like rubber mannequins with surprised eyes that stared—I felt like they stared at me. Others didn't have faces at all—completely blown off! Terrible—war is . . . there's nothing good about it, nothing noble, nothing valiant. It's a waste."

Caleb grimaced, as I imagined the upsetting images of war replayed in his mind.

"We were walking—strolling, really—through a rice paddy. I remember I was daydreaming about home. I was pretty homesick at that point; I'm not ashamed to say I really missed my mom. Her cooking. Her voice. Then—bang, bang, bang!—shots rang out. We're a few hundred yards from the base of Hill 19, and some Viet Cong sniper, from what direction I never learned, starts taking pot shots at us. Picking us off, one-by-one.

"It was chaos! I dove into the ankle-high water and began crawling. I heard men screaming, others shouting instructions. M-16s fired all around me. I never got a chance to pull the trigger. I scrambled on hands and knees toward Hill 19, climbing over dead Marines—my buddies—along the way."

Caleb pressed his lips together and closed his eyes, exhaled.

"Fifty yards—the width of a football field—from Hill 19 and I felt a scorching pain—like a bee sting times a million—in my back.

"I dropped into the water onto my belly, my nose and mouth just above the water. It took every bit of strength to turn over onto my back. When I did, it felt like a knife twisting in me—it took my breath away! Then the pain faded to nothing. I just lay there in the bloody water, the blazing sun baking me. I was thinking, 'This isn't happening to me. I'm not a 17-year-old Marine lying on my back in a rice paddy, bleeding to death in the middle of Vietnam. This isn't real.' I told myself, 'I'm six years old, this is the beach, my mom will bring me an ice cream soon.'"

Caleb paused. I saw tenderness in his features, like the face of a deer or some other sylvan soul.

"My mom always said that staring at the sun could blind you— that the sun's rays can shoot into your retinas and destroy them. But while lying in that rice paddy, I didn't care. I kept staring at the sun. There was a haze, like a halo—an angel's halo—surrounding it.

"Then it all slipped away—the splashing sounds, the ringing shots, the moans, screams, everything. It became silent, like I was deaf. And this will sound strange, but the only sound I heard was the sound of the sun."

Chapter Fourteen
SHEDDING MORE LIGHT

THE STORM HAD PASSED, leaving in its wake occasional winds that moved the verdant canopies above, gently shaking water from the broad leaves to the jungle under-story where Caleb and I sat cloistered and silent.

As I digested Caleb's words, I tried to imagine him lying half submerged in that rice paddy, looking up at the sun. The halo he saw as he stared into the sun, I identified with through my own experiences. Even the briefest gaze at the earth's star will create blotches of brightness that temporarily stay with the eyes, imprinting repeatedly like a shimmering stamp on all you see, but then fading with time. These shiny images are to the eyes, I suppose, what ringing is to the ears. What was the sound of the sun? Was it that high-pitched whistling that you hear when you're about to lose consciousness? Can it be described?

"It was high and low, loud and soft, brassy and muffled—all at once." Caleb read my incredulous look and blurted out, "I'm telling you exactly as I remember it! It was a heartbeat, it was a car crash, it was the buzzing of a bee, it was . . . everything and nothing in particular."

Caleb still had not bridged the gap between that day in Vietnam and his arrival on the island, so I waited for him to continue. He sat cross-legged, his right hand kneading his calf muscle, his eyes unblinkingly fixed upon the tangle of vinery and leaves in front of him; yet, fixed upon nothing. No doubt the water-blurred images from the past burned like a flickering candle in his mind.

"Caleb?"

My voice startled him; his eyes widened suddenly, his body jolted, as if roused from a deep sleep. "What's up, Pres?"

"You never finished your story—told how you arrived on this island."

"Right," began Caleb groggily. "How did you come to this island?"

"I have told you already," I said, calmly. "I washed ashore."

Caleb, still staring trance-like, scratched his whiskerless chin and then absentmindedly uttered, "Our routes were definitely different."

"How so?"

"I didn't get here by the sea . . . or by air, rail, flotsam, jetsam, car."

"How did you get here?"

"I don't know?" said Caleb, moving to his knees, and then rising into a standing position. The storm was now a memory, and only occasional droplets of water fell from the leaves and landed with a splat on the ground.

"Tell me what you do know—maybe I can make sense of it for you. And maybe it will help us find a way home?" I stood up.

"Right." Caleb smirked.

"Come on. Please explain."

Caleb looked defeated, exhausted. "There's not much to tell, Prescott. One moment I'm bleeding to death in a rice paddy in Vietnam, the sun is singing to me, burning my eyes, then I feel like I'm inside a lightning bolt—a blinding, noisy flash. And then," Caleb snapped his finger, "I'm here on this island . . . lying on my back . . . dry . . . uninjured."

"Where?"

"On a flat stone about a klick that way," Caleb pointed down the path in the direction away from the beach.

"Klick?"

"Kilometer."

"Kilometer?"

"Just walk that way, Pres." Caleb pointed again.

"You were bleeding to death?"

"I was bleeding to death."

"How can you be sure?

Caleb frowned. "I felt a sharp pain in my back, I saw blood in the water all around me . . . I'm sure."

"There were others injured around you," I stated. "It could have been their blood."

"Prescott!" Caleb breathed deeply, and then smiled. "Are you going to build another argument like your 'dodo case'?"

"All right," I said, ignoring his last remark. "What did you do then? Did you walk out to the beach?"

"No, I walked inland."

"Inland! And?"

"And the path led to a boardwalk of sorts, which led to a cave, which bore directly into the base of the volcano."

"Why not tell me this before?" I wasn't angry with Caleb, though the strain in my voice probably sounded so. I was disappointed that after spending nearly a month working and sleeping alongside him, he had kept these details to himself.

"I did tell you. I did. Think about it? You asked me why I didn't want to go inland and set up a shelter, and I told you the jungle was potentially more dangerous than a hurricane, did I not?"

"Yes, but . . ."

"You need proof, right? Seeing is believing?"

"Well . . ."

Caleb pointed down the path. "Walk about thirty minutes in that direction and get your proof."

"And what will I find beyond the cave?"

"Listen, little man, take a walk, investigate, and then come back and talk to me."

Caleb turned away and strode toward the hanging vines that blocked the view of the ocean.

"You're not coming with me?"

"Been there, done that," he called dismissively over his shoulder. "I'll talk to you later, Pres." Caleb pushed his body through the vines and walked into the brilliant sunshine. Then the vines drew back like a curtain and Caleb was gone.

Suddenly, I felt very alone.

When I reached the crest of the first hill, I glimpsed back at the distance I had traveled and then looked ahead at the narrowing, serpentine path. I leaned over, picked up a stick—roughly four feet in length and two inches in diameter—and then walked some more. The stick would serve as a walking stick, something to use if I needed to do any prodding and, if necessary, to use as a weapon for self-defense.

I could no longer smell the salt air, yet I gauged the beach was only a ten-minute walk—much less if I ran—away from me. I soon became so involved in my mind, replaying Caleb's story, that I hardly noticed my surroundings.

Did Caleb believe that he died on that rice paddy? Was he implying that at the moment when life gives way to the afterlife, he was spirited to this island on a bolt of lightning? If so, then what is this island to Caleb? Is it a holding station—a purgatory—for the dead? If so, where are the other spirits, the other dead?

I swallowed hard, and wondered if I would find the answer to my many questions on this journey.

Caleb dreaded the thought of traveling inland. After washing ashore on this island, I walked into the jungle and sensed something—a foreboding, a fear, and trepidation rippled like goose pimples across my body.

Why?

Caleb had survived being inland, and he just encouraged me to go look for myself. He was my friend. He would never purposely send me into a dangerous situation. And, if he thought there might be danger, he would have accompanied me. At least that is what I told myself.

Caleb and I had come to this island under the most random of circumstances. Reason advised me that even more random circumstances could remove me—a bird, perhaps, swooping in from the sky, grabbing me in its talons, and then carrying me to its aerie . . .

or a bolt of lightning electrifying my corporeal matter and spiriting me to another planet.

Awash in these thoughts and portents, I strode on, my heart in my throat, a walking stick in hand, and perspiration forming on my brow.

Chapter Fifteen
CANNON

THERE WAS SOMETHING DISCONCERTING about that hard-packed trail. It bothered my sensibilities. It nagged at me. Thick grasses and hardy shrubs hugged its edges, and an occasional root pierced its surface, but otherwise, the path was a smooth, dark skin of compressed earth.

My mind, making an association I did not understand immediately, suddenly pictured the Buckley Academy, which I had attended in England. Then I conjured up an image of a particular dog—an unsightly and corpulent black Labrador named Cannon—that used to waddle daily from house to house begging for victuals. This bloated canine had worn a winding path through the back garden of the academy—it being the middle point between the house of an old maid who doted on the dog and Mr. Worcester's house (A butcher by trade), who fed the dog scraps and trimmings carried home from his shop.

I remember quite distinctly that Cannon died in the winter of 1774. His passing aroused great sadness in the shire town, but I was not among the mourners, though I did miss the dog in a curious way. I had become dependent upon his routine—his multiple daily walks through the academy garden, along that well-worn path. The dog's uncomfortable, geriatric gait became a fixture in my life. The human condition adores routine, and so I missed old Cannon.

I did not miss the dog's personality (it was not distinguishable from any other dog's); I did not miss its bark (a hoarse whelp that sounded like he suffered from chronic whooping cough); and I did not miss the great piles of gelatinous feces piled along the garden in the most inconvenient locations (usually finding its way to the underside of my shoe). But I did miss Cannon's presence—its routine and my own had intersected.

The following spring, every time I glimpsed at the well-worn path, I thought of Cannon. That was also when I began to contemplate the life of the path. Would it survive in its current condition for another decade? I guessed so—and I guessed wrong. By August, grass had overtaken the greater portion of it. By September, a great growth of yellow weeds totally obscured it from view. By October, nothing remained of Cannon's magnum opus—only its shadowy memory.

My experience with cannon's path considered, I now looked at the jungle trail and reasoned that, unless trod upon constantly, plant life would quickly and completely obliterate it. In this fertile environment, the thick surrounding flora would release spores and seeds that would distribute along the path, and the nourishing daily afternoon rain and life-giving sunshine would raise the plants to healthy heights within thirty days. In short, the path would disappear.

So, why was it still here?

Simple: it was being used regularly.

Walked upon. Trod upon. Marched upon. Trampled. Beaten.

The next logical question: Who or what was maintaining the trail?

Perhaps the answer would soon reveal itself.

Chapter Sixteen
A WONDER

WHEN THE TRAIL TURNED LEFT NINETY DEGREES, I spied wooden posts in the shadowy distance.

"The boardwalk!" I said aloud, thinking of Caleb's description.

Closer still, I realized that weathered hemp rope lashed tombstone gray rails to vertical beams, which cast regular shadows on the perfectly level, arrow-straight timber walkway. This structure, which spanned a quarter of a mile, was intricately designed to smoothly pass over shallow wells and deep chasms in the volcanic rock. A boardwalk, it was not. It was a footbridge, barely wide enough for two men to walk abreast, built upon the undulating topography that molten lava, perhaps centuries ago, haphazardly sculpted.

I stopped where the hard-packed trail met the wooden tread boards of the footbridge. Whoever constructed it, with its teak hexagonal railings and crisscrossed support beams, did so with great care.

It was a marvel!

The wear on the center of each tread board was yet another physical reminder that humankind existed now or had existed recently on this island. I wondered, whose feet had walked upon this bridge? There was nary a soul in sight.

The great volcanic mount rose directly in front of me, black smoke rising as from a forge. I was at once terrified and deeply curious about entering a cave in that living mountain. I stood there, thinking, trying to will my legs to continue walking, to step upon the footbridge.

What if I was being watched?

I suddenly felt self-conscious, as if there were eyes observing me from behind the blended greens of the jungle foliage.

I heard a rustling above me, a distressed shriek, and then received a blow to the top of my head, then my shoulder, and then my head again and again. I dropped to the ground and curled into a ball, covering my head with my arms, but the pelting persisted. The once quiet jungle now erupted in noisy turmoil, as the manic shrieking multiplied to a deafening degree. I began to cry out, as each blow struck my body, and, though each strike smarted, it only felt as though a broom was hitting me. Nevertheless, I cried out each time, my eyes filled with tears, as I believed I was about to die.

The thumping abruptly stopped, but I waited and remained braced for another attack. The din continued, and sounded like a murder of crows screeching in my ears. When I perceived a reduction in the clamor, I peeked through my arms and discovered a mission of monkeys, all about the size of a cat, with yellowish-orange legs and arms, jumping up and down angrily on the footbridge in front of me. I sprung to my feet and backed away, glancing above me as I did to assure that no more of these prehensile-tailed rogues would drop from the foliage onto my aching head.

The agitated monkeys, more than fifty strong, continued to cry loudly as they displayed their great agility by leaping over one another, climbing the rails of the footbridge, and then springing off to branches overhead. I tried to move close to them, but they cried louder, bared their teeth at me, and began jumping up and down aggressively.

I picked up my walking stick, held it like a spear, and then furiously tossed it at the ten or so monkeys that remained blocking my way to the footbridge. The monkeys scattered, and the stick clanked onto the wooden treads of the bridge before rolling off, never to be seen again.

In a desperate rustling retreat, the monkeys traveled among the leaves, and their piercing wails attenuated as the distance between us increased.

I wiped the tears from my eyes and then jogged onto the footbridge. The tread boards thumped loudly under the weight of each footfall, startling me at first. Then, peering over my shoulder and seeing no more monkeys, I determined that it was safe to resume walking.

I felt an eerie calm as I strolled along that footbridge, and I began considering whether the sudden appearance of the monkeys had been cautionary—a forewarning. It was too strange, too calculated, I decided, to have been random. Each monkey purposely landed upon me, and then taunted me with chattering, sinister cries.

Tired of dwelling on monkeys, I tilted my head and arched my back to view the smoky tip of the mountain. This colossal and intimidating landmark loomed over me with quiet menace. I respected the power bubbling inside of it, a fiery cauldron capable of eradicating every living thing on the island and drastically changing the island's geography. The thought of finding and entering a cave in this potential bomb, as I had planned, did not sit well. Remembering how scared I had been when the *Serapis* began to engage in battle against the *Bonhomme Richard*, I gauged that my fear now was double that amount; after all, in battle my adversary had been a known entity, namely the British Navy, but God only knew who or what resided in the volcano.

So why did I keep walking? It is difficult to explain. I wouldn't say that I was drawn like a magnet or pulled as if by invisible strings toward the volcano, but there was an attraction, and alluring force at play that I did not understand.

The eyes can play tricks on you, and mine did as I resumed walking, all the while staring at the base of the volcanic mountain. I noticed a shadowed section against the rock that reminded me of a deep wrinkle on the hide of a huge beast. I focused on this shadow for quite a while as I moved toward it, and then I recognized in it a greater depth than my first impression supplied.

A cave!

The cave!

There was a short interruption of hard-packed trail after the footbridge, but then I stepped onto another wooden structure, a slightly inclined ramp, as I entered the dark cave. Yellow dots of flickering light illuminated at intervals small sections of the ramp. The sources of light, I realized, were burning torches, ensconced on the cave wall. I had never seen torches like these: the blue flames discharged upwards, like water unaffected by gravity, from horizontal copper piping that jutted from the smooth inner wall.

The presence of these magical torches bothered my sensibilities more than anything had since embarking on this minor journey, even more so than the truculent monkeys. Until I saw the lighted torches, I wanted to believe, despite the overwhelming evidence against it, that Caleb and I were the only inhabitants on the island. How could this still be true? The torches did not light themselves. They certainly had not been burning for centuries.

There I stood, statue-still in the unnatural flickering light, wondering, questioning—growing more afraid every minute. One of my favorite theories, that an ancient race of man once peopled this island, cultured in art, but unsophisticated in science, crumbled as I looked at the flames spitting from the copper tubes. Ancient men could have sculpted the statues on the beach and constructed the ramp that I stood upon, but these torches were either enchanted or the work of a living, breathing, sophisticated race of man, and I wondered whether I was being drawn into its nest, its lair.

The ramp, I soon realized, spiraled up through the dry sulfur air (think deviled eggs) of the cave. At one point, I leaned over an inside railing and looked down to gauge my progress. I could see snatches of the ramp illuminated by the many torches along the walls, and determined that I had traveled along the inner circumference of the cave, in a loose spiral.

After climbing for several more minutes, the texture beneath my shoes changed from smooth and solid to loose and granular. I knelt down and pulled up a handful of this material—fine and nearly weightless—like ashes. The darkness made it impossible for me to conclude whether it was soil, sand, or ash. I let the substance fall through my fingers to the ground, wiped my hands clean on my trousers, and then walked on.

I noticed a speck of light in the distance. I secured my eyes on this light, making it my beacon, and walked toward it. But the light did not grow in size the way a faraway object does when brought nearer, that is why, thinking that I was training my eyes on a distant spot of light, I was startled to suddenly and violently reach an end. My feet found a stone wall before my head did, thankfully. And then and there, my nose touching the dusty stonewall, I got my bearings. To my right was another copper-pipe torch burning more brightly than any I had seen before. Its light had reflected in a shiny surface, perhaps mica, along the wall that my nose pressed against. I had mistaken this reflection for a light source, just as children often mistake the moon's reflection of the sun for a light source.

I turned to my right and began walking toward this great torch, and once beyond its blinding glare, I saw a great opening emitting streaming rays of diffuse natural white light.

"Am I through?" I said aloud to myself, and then began walking toward the great, bright opening, which I assumed exited out of the cave into the equatorial sunlight.

A great breeze blew in from the lighted area, pushing back my hair and drying the perspiration on my skin. The air lifted past me, no doubt rising to an unseen opening high above. Moving closer, the rocks around me converged, creating a misty burst of light in the niche between two rocky walls. I squeezed past a particularly narrow section and beheld a marvelous set of carved stairs.

I descended four steps, the fresh air streaming past me, the bright white light enveloping me.

And there in front of me was a wonder.

Chapter Seventeen
LOVE AND DEATH

I STOOD UPON A STUNNING SPIRAL STAIRCASE the color of ivory that unwound downward into the whitest, brightest room I have ever seen. Pristine marble, the color of snow and with the sheen of polished silver, covered every surface of this small chamber. Four alabaster columns surged upward into the streaming sunlight, and as I placed my black shoes onto the glimmering marble floor, I spied thick emerald vines wrapped around the columns like sleeping serpents basking in the tropical sunlight.

I studied my lightly reflected inverted image in the shimmering surface of the marble floor, and slowly turning on a point—my shoes clacking against the hard surface—examined the bare chamber. Then gazing skyward again, I marveled at the great shafts of white light shooting down from small openings in the vaulted ceiling. Particles of dust floating in these beams of light swayed and swirled like dancing ghosts as I walked past. Beyond the farthest column I discovered an archway that led into another chamber bathed in white sunlight. Walking beneath this archway, I left behind what I determined was a portico, and entered a great hall of equal luminescence.

My heart throbbed in my chest as I baby-stepped into this great hall. I first heard the plashing of agitated water, and then saw a circular pool at the center of the room, out of which two jets of water spurted upwards to three times my height and, at the apex, lay suspended in air for a moment before turning inward and then trickling down upon itself in thick droplets.

I quickly scanned the room and determined that I was alone, though I still stepped forward haltingly, the hair on my neck standing on end like a frightened cat, as my senses desperately gathered information from my surroundings and prepared for the worst.

Moving closer to the pool with the twinjets, I suddenly recognized a human form to my right. My heart became a pair of kettledrums alternately pounding out two distinct low tones that resonated in my ears.

I leapt back in surprise.

He leapt back.

I lowered my head like a dog and stood in a defensive stance.

He did the same.

I exhaled, rose to my full height, and then laughed ashamedly.

He did the same—he who stood my own height, kept his dark hair pulled back in a ribbon-pinched ponytail, and wore blue breeches above light calf-high stockings and black shoes.

It was my reflection in a wall of smoky glass.

I was now clammy and breathless, my heartbeat irregular, and my gut feeling scrambled and loose, like a disemboweled animal. I wanted to rest on the edge of the fountain, and I would have if I had not seen hanging on the bleach-white marble wall to the left of the twin-jetted pool two colorful tapestries, massive in scale.

Each tapestry depicted nearly identical figures, young men in richly embroidered golden robes, standing against the reddish background. One broad-stroked English word, inked black and italicized, loomed ominously below each of these mysterious forms. The first tapestry read, "Love." The second read, "Death." Beneath Love's curly brown locks were a broad forehead, straight nose and a slightly upturned mouth—more of a simper that gave it an arrogant, self-assured air. Death's features were similar, but he did not smile— his blood red mouth was a grave horizontal slit. Each flinty-eyed figure held a wreath of withered flowers, and scores of loosened lilac-colored petals cascaded unhappily downward. Slightly obscured in the center of the wreath that Death held was a human skull in front profile, the dark eye-sockets peering blankly ahead.

"What does it all mean?" I asked aloud.

I turned around to face the fountain, and that is when I noticed a large oval door with a golden knob strangely placed at its center. I felt both drawn and repulsed by this portal, and I think my curiosity would have propelled me forward and convinced me to turn the knob if my ears had not detected a stray, high-pitched sound.

Laughter.

Chilling fairy laughter. Did it ride the sunlight into the room? It reverberated against the hard surfaces of this great hall, chattered like the taunting cries of the monkeys. And then, like water being poured into a vessel, the dread filled my toes and legs and torso until it came spilling out of my mouth in the form of a brief screech.

And, like a church sexton snuffing a candle, all noise immediately ceased—even the twinjets dropped like a dead man and lay motionless in the untroubled water.

The kettledrums returned to my ears, pounding and pounding and pounding. My eyes flashed left and right, as I spun in a circle, my shoes echoing like handclaps above the stifling silence. I grew scared for my life, as I sensed a sinister presence near—as though some predatory animal, drool dripping from its fanged mouth, scrutinized me from some hidden niche.

I sprinted across the great hall, beneath the archway, and into the portico. I leapt up the ivory stairs and then entered the darkness of the cave, frantically feeling my way along the uneven wall of stone.

Moments later, I was jogging down the spiraling ramp, blood pumping in all my extremities. I did not look back, and never stopped running my fastest, until I reached the opening of the cave, where I reduced to a quick jog across the footbridge, constantly surveying the trees above for monkeys, but hardly noticing what I passed on either side.

When I reached the hard-packed path that I knew would lead me to the beach and back to the campsite on the plateau, I slowed to a quick walk. Moments later, it seemed, I was pushing aside the whirling vines and walking with much difficulty across the sandy beach. My throat was dry, and sweat poured out of my hair, stinging my eyes.

"Wait one minute!" I said to myself, and immediately turned around to face the stone statues that I had just passed between. "Love and Death," I whispered. I moved closer, studied the faces, and sure enough there was an unmistakable facial resemblance to the figures on the great hall tapestries. Not only that, one statue held flowers, the other a human skull. "Who are you?" I asked the statue holding the skull. "And what do you symbolize?"

Later, as I nearly finished climbing the familiar path that ascended to our encampment on the plateau, I saw black smoke rising from the campfire before I saw Caleb. He stood with his back to me, both hands resting on his hips, staring at his battle helmet, which hung on an improvised wooden frame above the fire.

"A watched pot never boils," I remember shouting, taking a shallow breath between nearly every word.

Caleb casually turned and showed that smug grin that I understood expressed feigned disapproval.

"What?"

"Prescott," he said sleepy-eyed. "I'd like to introduce you to Julian Woodgate."

Following an imaginary line that his outstretched arm and pointed index finger started, my eyes moved in the direction of the hooch.

What did I see?

A very tall man I did not recognize, fast asleep on my palm-leaf bed, wearing a green military uniform and curious black boots.

Chapter Eighteen
WORRYING

"WHO . . .? WHEN DID HE . . .?" I did not know where to begin.

"A couple of hours ago—just after I left you." There was no concern in Caleb's voice; actually, he appeared bored as he leisurely squatted down and then sat on the sand, his back leaning against a boulder. He stretched out his left leg, and rested his ropey-veined forearm over the knee of the drawn up right leg. He looked at me through dirty spectacles, his head tilted, and wearing his characteristic miniature smirk, which was a lifting of one side of the mouth and the raising of one cheek.

I stole a quick glance toward the sleeping man and then quickly moved into a sitting position to the left of Caleb, a spot I purposely chose because it afforded me a clear view of the sleeping stranger. "What is he?" I asked in a whisper.

"He's a man, Prescott," said Caleb in a booming voice. "What do you think?"

"I know he is a man," I said, whispering. "But what kind of a man is he? You know—where is he from? What time?"

"It's a little after three o'clock, I would guess," said Caleb in an impassive matter-of-fact manner.

"Caleb!" I screeched his name and then quickly checked to confirm that my voice had not disturbed the sleeping man.

Caleb laughed. "I found him unconscious on the beach, Pres. The bugger was facedown in the sand, so I picked him up and carried him here."

I lifted my chin and scrutinized the man though squinted eyes. "He is sleeping, right? Not—"

"No, no—he's not dead. He spoke to me after I put him in the hooch."

"Spoke? What language?"

"English. He mumbled something about mortars, Germans, and other weird junk."

"Is that how you learned his name?"

Caleb shook his head. "No, I read his tags."

My urge at that moment was to blurt out everything I had seen inland, my adventures, the fairy laughter, the monkeys, the fountains and tapestries, the door . . . but I did not, for some reason. Instead, Caleb and I remained unusually quiet for several minutes.

I grasped onto my ankles and held my legs against my chest, my chin resting on my knees, sitting lost in thought. I thought of an old saying that I heard many times growing up: "Misery loves company." Did I believe it? My first impulse was that I did not. For instance, I was trapped on a nowhere land, a potentially dangerous island, a place where time had little or no meaning, often scared, confused, sad; yet, I suddenly felt compassion for the sleeping man, knowing that he would soon wake to learn he was a million miles and a million lifetimes away from the place he called home. Mulling it over, though, I decided that this was not a misery loves company situation, because, despite it all, I did not feel miserable.

I stood up, tiptoed to the hooch, and gazed down at the sleeping man. He appeared Caleb's age, twenty years old at most. His hair, neatly parted to the side, was short in length. He had an opossum face: a long pointed nose, narrow lips, and a weak chin. His skin was pale and smooth, and his ears stuck out ninety-degrees from his head and resembled the handles on a jug.

He lay on his back, with his hands clasped at the waist. His greenish gray uniform jacket had a leather belt around the midsection and, radiating diagonally from the belt, a black leather strap that threaded through what Caleb later told me was an epaulet on his right shoulder. He was tall and lean, which impelled Caleb to later remark that "he could hide behind the legs of a stork."

He was certainly alive: I watched his chest rise and fall calmly beneath his clasped white hands.

I returned to Caleb, now working on something he had been planning to do for several weeks: building a bench. "Enough sitting in the sand or on rocks," he had said a few days ago. "This camp needs some furniture." Kneeling in the sand, he used vines to tie together six trimmed branches, each about four or five inches in diameter, to create the seat of his bench. Resting on the ground behind him were two large logs that he must have carried to the camp while I was gone inland.

"The sleeping man is from a time near your own time," I said.

"I know," said Caleb, as he dug a hole in the sandy ground with the metal excavation shovel. Satisfied with the depth, he rolled one of the logs into the hole, used his bare feet to push sand into the hole, and then walked around the log in what looked like an Indian dance, in order to tamp the sand down.

"He is your age," I said, trying to make conversation.

"I know," said Caleb, digging another hole.

"Where do you think he is from?"

Caleb, sweating in the afternoon sun, dragged the second log into the hole and followed the same routine as he did with the first log. Finished, Caleb smiled brightly, but did not make eye contact with me. "I know where he's from. He's your enemy, Prescott."

Caleb lifted the bundled branches and placed them on the logs, and his bench was completed. "Ta-da!" he said.

"Caleb, what do you mean—my enemy?" I gazed over at the sleeping man, eager to learn what Caleb knew. He did not look dangerous, and I could not for the life of me think of why he would be considered my enemy.

The wood creaked as Caleb sat down on the bench. "Looks like it'll hold," he said. "All three of us should fit—you, me, and your enemy."

"Why won't you tell me what you are talking about?" I said, in a hushed voice. Now sprawled out flat on the bench, his bare chest to the sun, his eyes closed, an exaggerated smile on his face, his hands behind his head, Caleb looked as though he were relaxing in a hammock.

"Caleb?" I whined.

"He's British, Prescott," he said, finally. "You know, from that dreaded place called England?"

My heart sank.

"What? Do you think he will mean me any harm?"

"Absolutely not."

"Are you certain?" I whispered.

"I'm certain."

"How so?"

"Because he lived during a time when America and England were allies."

"Allies?"

"They fought together against the Germans—in 1916, if my history serves me right—in World War One."

"1916?"

"In 1916."

"He will not want to harm me?"

"Not unless you drive him crazy with your constant questions." Caleb opened an eye and smiled at me.

"Good," I said, and exhaled.

"Hey!" said Caleb, as I pushed his feet off of the bench. "What are you doing?"

"You are on my side of the bench." I sat down next to Caleb.

"This thing will even hold a tub-of-lard like you." Caleb joked as he patted my scrawny midsection.

"If I am lard then you are a pregnant cow." I lightly punched Caleb's rippling gut.

"Oh yeah, well this pregnant cow might just crush you," said Caleb as he leapt onto me.

"Ouch! Caleb," I said giggling. "You are breaking my legs!"

Caleb then stood on the bench and began wiggling his backside against my turned-away head. "Maybe you'd prefer the soft pillow that I call my butt!"

"Get that smelly thing away from me, you pig!" I yelled between rippling laughter. In fact, we both laughed, squawked like birds, and released all manner of decorum.

Suddenly, Julian Woodgate sat up straight and scowled at us.

Our laughter stopped, and the hissing of the waves below and the riffling of the palm leaves in the breeze returned.

Time seemed frozen, and then I watched the expressions on the man's face change from curiosity to bewilderment to fear to anger to amusement and back round again, no doubt influenced by each new thought and theory in his head. He was trying to get his bearings, to place our faces in his memory, to make sense of the new surroundings. But our faces and this island were not in his memory. We lived outside of his memory, in a place that is not the future and not the past.

The man smiled—a confused smile. The grogginess was wearing off.

"I say," he finally spoke, his voice low and booming, "Where on God's earth am I?" the man said examining the hooch. "And who are you two? And why are you making such an infernal racket?"

Chapter Nineteen
AWAKENING

JULIAN WOODGATE CRAWLED OUT OF THE TENT and then unfolded his long, skinny limbs into a standing position; rising to a greater height than Caleb first surmised (Woodgate later informed us he was 6 feet, 4 inches tall). I walked toward him with my right hand extended to offer a welcoming handshake. I was eager to get off to a good start, especially because I feared he might hold a grudge against my countrymen and me. Interestingly, it was not until much later when it occurred to me that Caleb and I were fellow countrymen. Perhaps I did not realize this because I had been plucked away at a time when Massachusetts Colony was neither English nor American. It was its own island in history—a no-man's land in time.

"You are on an island, sir," I said, answering his question and introducing myself. He accepted my outstretched hand, leaned down, gripped it firmly, giving two quick pumps, and then released it. I studied his face for the first time. His pale blue eyes were kind, but somewhat doleful. His teeth appeared in decent condition—but inferior to the sparkling enamel in Caleb's mouth.

"An island?" he said in a gruff voice, which produced a low, rasping sound and made the listener sympathetically clear his own throat. "Good God, boy," he said. "What island?" Woodgate peered over my shoulder at Caleb, who lay supine on the bench, his hands across his chest like a prepared corpse. "You there—what is your name?"

"Caleb Thompson, private first class, United States Marine Corps, sir!" he said, feigning enthusiasm, his eyes closed as he spoke.

"This is Bedlam if it is anything," Woodgate said to himself. Then, in a louder voice, he called to Caleb: "Can you tell me the coordinates of this island, location, anything useful?"

"Prescott," said Caleb. "Give him the coordinates, will you?"

Woodgate turned to me, a stony expression on his face.

"I," I stammered, shrugging my shoulders to show that I did not have the answer to his question. "You have to understand, Caleb is a wag—he jests all the time." I forced a smile, but felt very uncomfortable, and no doubt blushed as I internally censured myself for acting like a pudding head.

Woodgate turned to the oblivious Caleb basking in the sun, and then walked to the edge of the cliff, showing his back to us.

I watched as this man looked out at the sea, no doubt searching for answers among the waves and winging gulls and nebulous fair-weather clouds. His shoulders rose and then fell, and then he placed his hands like two anchors into his trouser pockets before turning to face me.

"You," he said pointing his finger at me. "You are wearing a sailor's garb, from the 18th century, are you not?"

I examined my canvas knee breeches and light stockings. "I am," I said.

"Why?" He now hovered over me, looking down his long nose.

"Well, sir," I began. "It is because I am from that time."

"Really?" he said, sarcastically. "You look very well for your advanced age." He patted me on the head patronizingly. "Why, you must be one hundred and fifty years old!" His vigorous laughter trailed off as soon as he realized he was the only one laughing. Then he looked crossly at Caleb and me.

"Prescott's age all depends on who you ask," said Caleb, suddenly up and around, placing dried sticks on the campfire.

"It shouldn't matter whom I ask!" said Woodgate, squaring his shoulders toward Caleb. "I only ask that you be courteous and provide me with an honest answer."

Caleb moved in front of Woodgate, who, though couple of inches taller, was only half the man. Caleb's chest now pressed against Woodgate's, a gesture whose aim was intimidation. Woodgate, however, did not flinch. Each man stood his ground, staring unblinkingly into the other's eyes.

"How about you be courteous and not call my friend a liar!" Caleb held each hand in a fist at his sides, his colossal chest expanded.

"I only ask for the truth," Woodgate said between gritted teeth.

"I'll give it to you straight right now. You ready to listen?"

Woodgate nodded.

"Prescott is 200 years older than me. You—you're old enough to be my grandfather."

"You're mad," said Woodgate, backing away. "I recently celebrated my nineteenth birthday."

"Ha! Don't expect any more birthday celebrations," said Caleb as he turned and sauntered toward his newly constructed bench.

"Is that a threat?" said Woodgate, in a forceful voice. Woodgate turned toward me, "Is he threatening me?"

I stood there dumbly, kicking at the sand and shrugging my shoulders.

Woodgate brought his thumb up to his mouth and tapped its knuckle against his chin a couple of times. "Very good, chap," he said, putting his hands down at his side and straightening. "I'll play along." He took several steps toward Caleb. "This boy is an eighteenth century sailor and you—what are you? That is, what are you besides American." Woodgate spat out the word "American."

"I already told you, Woody," said Caleb, buttoning his green shirt. "I am a Marine."

"You are dressed unlike any American Marine I have seen," said Woodgate, softening his approach.

"That's because the Marines you fought with were not born in 1950 like me," said Caleb, pushing up his spectacles with his index finger.

Woodgate's perplexed expression—the scrunching of his eyebrows, the squinting of his eyes, the lifting of his right cheek— entertained me, as did the way his head moved back and forth, like a cat captivated by a clock's pendulum: he studied me, then studied Caleb and then studied me again. Then a sheepish smile gradually appeared on his face, and he began wagging his long forefinger. "Very good, men," he said, exhaling. "You are jesting. You've had your fun." Caleb smiled broadly. He obviously derived so much joy from this poor man's confusion, and watching Caleb, the wily tomcat toying with a mouse, stirred great mirth in me. I clearly understood that quality in Caleb that enjoyed being the center of attention and the hub of confusion.

Caleb offered Woodgate his hand to shake, which Woodgate accepted. "Come with me, Woody," said Caleb, and then led him toward the edge of the cliff.

Woodgate's eyes sparkled merrily, as he turned and walked with Caleb. I followed the two men and stood by and listened as Caleb spoke.

"Look out there," Caleb said, his hand outstretched toward the horizon, "and search the sea. In your mind build a ship and sail on it. Where were you stationed?"

"France," said Woodgate.

"OK," Caleb said. "Sail that ship to France. Get out, eat some snails and some cheese, and then go to where you fought. You follow?"

Woodgate nodded.

"Do you know what you'll find there?" Caleb did not wait for a response. "I'll tell you what you won't find. You won't find the battlefields of France out there. Why? Because they're history. Gone. Sure, you can find the towns, the land where you stood, but the trenches, those endless dog-toothed trenches, they're all filled in and likely covered in green grass."

When Caleb mentioned the dog-toothed trenches, something in Woodgate's expression changed from amusement to concern.

"As a matter of fact," continued Caleb, placing his hand over Woodgate's bony shoulder, "your side won the war, if it means anything to you. But then Hitler and the Nazis took over power and we went back to war against the Germans in the 1940s—at least America did. I think the Brits joined the war earlier."

Woodgate put his hands in the pockets of his trousers; his narrow shoulders slouched and his head sank.

"You know, Mr. Woodgate," I said, moving next to him. "We really need your help. Caleb has been here nearly two months, and I have been here three weeks . . . and . . . we want to go home."

Woodgate lifted his chin, turned his head, and looked down his nose at me. "If what you say is true, and we are on some timeless island where people from across the centuries are thrown together, then I am afraid that I cannot likely help you."

Caleb winked and smiled at me, then subtly motioned with his head for me to follow him. When we were about fifteen feet away and heading toward the path that led to the beach, Caleb whispered, "Let's give him some time to adjust. We don't want to smother him."

I realized the logic in this notion. I remembered needing time on my own to sort out the unusual situation.

Caleb turned to Woodgate, shouted that we would return in an hour's time, reached for his green canvas bag, and then we continued down the path.

We filled that hour gathering fresh fruit and water. Then Caleb, using the spear that he kept beneath a thick evergreen bush at the upper part of the beach, managed to spear four white bass of considerable size in what he termed "record time."

I used this opportunity, as Caleb fished, to tell him all that had occurred when I traveled inland. Caleb listened intently, occasionally nodding with a knowing smile whenever I mentioned something he had seen too. But Caleb's nodding acknowledgments ceased when I described the portico with the milk-white marble. I learned that he had not traveled that far into the cave.

When I described the second room, which I referred to as the great hall, and mentioned the twin-jetted fountain and the tapestries with the depictions of the two young men—Love and Death— Caleb's eyes widened and his mouth slackened.

And when I told him about the door that I did not explore, the high-pitched childish laughter I heard, how the fountain's jet suddenly died, he nearly jumped out if his own skin.

"Woah!" he said, snapping his head back. "Just when I was getting settled here—getting used to the cards I'd been dealt . . . and now you tell me this."

"I speak only the truth, Caleb," I said.

"Man, I don't doubt you, believe me." He shook his head and cracked a wry smile. "It's just—wow!"

Caleb placed the last of the four white bass into his green rucksack, and then slung it over his shoulder.

"Caleb," I said. "I thought that we—you and I—should make a trip inland together and explore further. Who knows, it may . . ."

"Are you nuts?" Caleb said. "And get attacked, killed or . . . worse?"

After spending so much time as I had with Caleb, I understood his tendency to react, then ruminate, and then, finally, reason. Therefore, I believed he was in stage one of the process. I spoke no more about it, allowing him ample quiet time to think about what I had said. I carried fruit, which I bundled in the front tails of my shirt. Caleb carried the rucksack with the fish inside, and we ascended the trail, leaving behind a large wooden bowl that Caleb had fashioned out of a log to carry water back from the spring.

When we returned to the plateau, Woodgate sat on the sand with his back against a large boulder; it was my favorite sitting spot. He watched us carry the fruit and fish, which we placed on the palm leaves in our hooch to keep the burning late afternoon sun from drying our supper.

Caleb skipped down the path in a slow trot to retrieve the container of fresh water while I threw more wood on the fire. The sun was low in the sky.

"We are going to have a feast, Mr. Woodgate," I said, trying to kindle a conversation.

He looked over at me doubtfully and then stood up and said, "I suppose that we should feast before getting feasted upon."

Chapter Twenty
BURYING

CRISIS WILL MAKE BROTHERS OF ENEMIES. To say that Woodgate and Caleb were enemies, though, would be too strong a sentiment, but it did not go unnoticed by me that each man eyed the other with suspicion and disapproval during our quiet dinner on Woodgate's first evening. The conversation was polite and guarded, which was a great struggle for the irreverent Caleb whose favorite subjects include the privy, belching, and puns about the buttocks of animals. By dinner's end, we knew little or nothing about Woodgate, other than that he was British and 19 years of age. Caleb inferred from his proper way of speaking, the way he formed his words at the back of his throat, that he was from a wealthy upbringing and likely well educated, which made me proud to hear, because I believed my own way of speaking was closer to Woodgate's than it was to Caleb's.

The day was waning, gasping above the roiling sea. Taking a cue from the plummeting sun, Caleb rose and walked to the edge of the cliff where each evening he enjoyed witnessing "the great ball of fire dipping into the horizon." I followed Caleb's long shadow to Woodgate, who pulled a small leathern book from the inside of his coat and began flipping through the pages. It was a moment of calm, of repose.

Then crisis.

"Prescott!" Caleb shouted. "Hurry! Come take a look!"

I rushed over next to Caleb and tried to follow the rest of the imaginary line that his outstretched arm began. Woodgate, startled by Caleb's shouting, also jumped to his feet and stood next to us, peering out into the ocean.

"Do you see that light?" Caleb asked, excitedly. "There! I see a swatch of orange. No, now—there! About a quarter of the way to the horizon—do you see?"

"No," I said.

"I see it," said Woodgate, calmly. "Something is bobbing on the waves. I see it. Now I don't. Now I do. What is it?"

"I can't make it out," said Caleb. "And now I don't see it."

I scoured the waves with my eyes, frantically eager to see what Woodgate and Caleb saw, but could only spy white caps, dark patches of sea, and spurts of agitated water slapping against submerged rocks.

"There again!" yelled Caleb. "It's a life vest—an orange life vest! There's a man down there!" Caleb turned quickly and bolted down the hill that led away from our camp.

I immediately began running after Caleb. "Wait up!" I implored, but he did not slow.

Ten minutes later I was on the beach, standing ankle-deep in the waves, now with only the lunar glow as a light source. The sea was calm tonight, but the approaching waves made a loud enough din that I knew Caleb would not hear my shouts, so I quieted and waited. Woodgate eventually caught up to me. It seemed that nothing he did was in haste. Perhaps it required extra effort to unravel those long limbs.

I spied a blinking red light, and pointed it out to Woodgate. The light was moving toward us, and I suddenly felt very afraid. Woodgate backed up a few paces.

"Woodgate! Prescott!" called Caleb, as he appeared out of the darkness. "Come here and give me a hand."

I rushed forward until the water was nearly up to my chin. Woodgate moved in beyond me, and I watched as he and Caleb, now standing around the blinking red light, began struggling with a large object. Each man then flanked this object and began making quick work of hauling it ashore.

I backed up until I was chest deep in the water and waited for them to bring in their catch—this blinking red treasure. I have to admit that I was at a complete loss as to what this object might be, even though Caleb had first pronounced it a man. I could associate nothing from my past with what I was seeing. To me it was an amorphous dark-thing with a blinking red light attached.

The splashing, the rushing and retreating of the waves, the quick movement of the two men's legs and arms, the heavy breathing accompanying the great struggle and effort, and the blinking of the red light—it was a blur of motion and confusion.

"Pres!" yelled Caleb. "Get over here and hold his head up out of the water!"

"What?" I said, almost as soon as I realized what they carried was a middle-aged man, seemingly strapped to a large wooden object.

The man's head hung limply over the edge of this flat wooden board, occasionally dipping into the sea. I grasped his soaking hair and then cupped my hands under his head to provide support. And it was like this, Woodgate and Caleb clutching the sides of this wooden plank that supported the man, and me cradling his head, that we brought him out of the sea and onto the beach.

Caleb and Woodgate then worked frantically to detach this man, who was bound to the wooden board with cords of a very unusual elasticized material—Caleb called them bungee cords, a term that Woodgate and I were unfamiliar with. The red light continued to blink, and upon closer inspection I realized that it was attached to a bright, bulky orange vest that the man wore.

Caleb pulled out his large knife, cut the strap on the man's chest, pulled away the vest and the red light, and then threw it several feet farther up the beach. Caleb then leaned in and placed his head against the man's chest.

"He's not breathing!" he said. "We'll have to do mouth-to-mouth"

"Mouth-to-mouth?" Woodgate asked, confused.

Caleb pressed his lips against the man's lips, pinched the man's nose with his left hand, and began blowing air into his lungs. Then he turned the man's head and pressed on his chest with great force. Caleb repeated this procedure several more times. Finally, he put his ear to the man's chest and then looked up at Woodgate and me, who were standing there as still as scarecrows. "He's gone."

Caleb stood up, rubbed his hands together, and then wiped them on his trousers. He looked down at the dead man and then at the blinking red light a few paces away.

"He's likely been dead a while," he said.

"What do you think happened to him?" said Woodgate.

"It's tough to say," said Caleb. "But if I had to guess I would say that he crashed a small plane, a Cessna or something lightweight, into the sea."

"How do you know he was in an aeroplane?" asked Woodgate.

"He is wearing a pilot's uniform," said Caleb. "The orange and black patches on the shoulders of his white button-up shirt tell me he was a commercial pilot, but there is no insignia on his shirt to indicate that he worked for a big airline, so it is unlikely that he flew a commercial jumbo jet."

"You can tell all that from his clothing?" I said, impressed by Caleb's inferences.

"Of course," said Caleb, who then walked over to the wooden plank. "He must have known he was crashing and hurriedly put on the life vest with that emergency light, and then found this piece of flotsam in the sea and strapped himself to it."

A patch of thick clouds blotted out the moon, and it was now very dark, but I could tell that the wooden flotsam, which was about six feet long and three feet wide, was made of several pieces joined together by a carpenter, and therefore I conjectured that it must have once been part of a larger construction, perhaps from a wrecked ship. This dead man and I arrived on this strange island by a similar means, a point that, at the time, meant very little to me.

"Where is he from?" I asked, returning my eyes to the dead man.

"I don't know," said Caleb.

"Your time?" I wondered.

"No," said Caleb, scratching his head. "From a time after me. Look at this." Caleb leaned down and pulled the metallic wristwatch from the man's arm. "Look at the display," he said, as Woodgate and I leaned in to examine the watch. "It has no hands—only numbers. Ten fifty-four. I've never seen such a thing before."

"Neither have I," said Woodgate, softly.

"Here then," said Caleb, tossing the watch to him. "It's yours. Keep it. He doesn't need it anymore."

Woodgate caught the watch, but I could tell by his down-turned mouth and widened eyes that he would have felt more comfortable holding a diseased rat.

Afraid that leaving the man above ground would attract animals, Caleb suggested we bury him immediately. Woodgate and Caleb carried the man to the highest point on the beach, where the jungle and beach meet. Caleb retrieved his metal excavation shovel from the hooch and then quickly dug a shallow grave. He and Woodgate gently placed the body in the grave, I folded the man's arms across his chest, and then Caleb began tipping shovelfuls of sand into the grave. I placed a large stick in the ground to mark the grave, and promised to return in the morning to construct a proper marker, a crucifix made of wood.

When the last shovelful of sand brought the grave level with the rest of the beach, Caleb retreated a few steps and Woodgate stepped forward clasping his hands. He then bowed his head and spoke: "We know not your name, your home, or your intended destination. We only know that you died before your time, which is always a shame. May God bless you on your final journey home."

Chapter Twenty-One
CODEBREAKING

MY FATHER ONCE TOLD ME SOMETHING that I have turned over in my mind ever since I arrived on this island. He told me, "How you live depends on your relationship with death." I first interpreted this as a lesson on morals, meaning that all God-fearing mortals should live life in a way that will pass the eternal judgment of God. The Ten Commandments immediately came to mind, as I ticked through the list of things I had not done, including stealing, dishonoring my mother and father, murdering—though I fear that I had not kept the Sabbath holy on more occasions than I cared to count. After all, a quick bathe down by the docks of the Boston Harbor on some of the hottest Sundays in the summer seemed a small infraction, and I justified swimming as a form of baptism, though I know that the Lord might not consider sacred the wrestling, splashing, and diving for imagined treasure with the other Sabbath-breakers (mostly apprentices my own age who toiled for local coopers, chandlers, tinsmiths).

But, here on this Godforsaken island, as Caleb referred to it, I could not avoid thinking in new terms. If this was the afterlife or another dimension of time or an extension of life, then my relationship with death certainly had changed. If this was a second chance at life, then I wanted to make the most of it. Death was what I wanted to avoid, even if it is a paradise, an Eden.

These thoughts and more ran hurry-scurry across my mind as the friendly rays of morning sunlight tiptoed on cat's paws across the night-cooled sand. I lay on my back with my arms behind my head, only a few yards away from the smoldering campfire, where I had spent the night beneath the expanse of stars, breathing in a pleasing admixture of jungle and sea smells, and thinking about all that had occurred the day before: the day Woodgate arrived and the day we buried the mysterious man with the ability to fly on the air.

Woodgate, who slept on my bed, rose early and walked past me wearing only a light shirt and his underclothes. I noticed that his bird-like legs, pasty white and nearly hairless, were the opposite of Caleb's muscular, hairy, and tanned limbs.

"You want to put some pants on, Woody?" Caleb said later that morning. "I'd like to eat breakfast without being blinded by the reflection off of those sticks you call legs."

Woodgate, who was now seated near the newly stoked fire, raised an eyebrow, but did not remove his eyes from the leathern book that he held in front of him. "I should think you would have better things to do with your time than to obsess over my legs," said Woodgate, a smirk appearing and then disappearing from his face.

"I have all the time in the world, Woody," said Caleb, completely indifferent to Woodgate's taunt.

"I am glad to see you in better spirits, Mr. Woodgate," I said, still retaining the title before his name. For some reason, though we learned he was only 19 years of age, he seemed much older than Caleb, and my upbringing taught me to respect my elders.

I later pondered why I did not use a title when speaking with Caleb and concluded that, despite our difference in age, Caleb felt like my peer; that . . . and the one time after I said "sir" to Caleb, he threatened to give me a "wedgie," if I did so again. Naturally, I was confused about whether this was a good or bad thing, until he explained that wedgies were a lifting of one's undergarments until they collect in a most uncomfortable way in-between the cleft in your buttocks. I never again called him sir.

"Thank you, Prescott," said Woodgate. "I am in better spirits, though I know not why."

"Here," said Caleb, who walked by Woodgate and threw down trousers and a long-sleeved shirt on the sand next to him. "The sun is strong here. Put your clothes on, unless you want to look like a Maine lobster."

Woodgate gathered his clothes, stood up, and began putting on his gray trousers. "Right-o, good man. Thank you."

"No problem, good man," said Caleb, mimicking Woodgate's accent.

Woodgate was now buttoning his heavy gray shirt, and then I watched as he rolled up the sleeves just above his elbows. "So what will it be today, gentlemen?" asked Woodgate. "Will there be another corpse lashed to a board, floating upon the sea? Perhaps a man from space will parachute onto our encampment today?"

At that moment I looked into the sky, fearful that just such a scenario would play itself out.

Caleb, holding a bunch of bananas in his left hand, bit into a banana that he held in his right hand as he sat down cross-legged next to me and across from Woodgate. "So, Woody," began Caleb. "You're ready to talk now."

Woodgate shook his head, looking confused by this statement, "I have always been ready to talk."

"Good," said Caleb, who then threw a banana at Woodgate, causing him to drop his leathern book in order to catch the fruit. "Where were you fighting in France?"

"Fighting?" Woodgate reached down, picked up his book, and with a down-turned mouth, began carefully wiping the sand from its cover.

"During the Great War, as you call it," said Caleb.

"And what do you call it?" Woodgate said, the smirk returning to his face.

"World War I, Woody," said Caleb.

Woodgate's eyes widened at this statement, no doubt because it implied that additional world wars had followed, wars that he could know nothing about.

"I was on the front line," said Woodgate.

"Infantry?"

Woodgate shook his head. "No, I did not carry a gun."

"You were on the front line and you didn't carry a gun," said Caleb, grinning. "What did you do, throw rocks?"

Woodgate carefully placed the leathern book into his large shirt pocket. "I was a code breaker. I intercepted messages and decoded them."

"Really?" said Caleb, leaning forward with interest. "You must be a pretty smart guy. You speak more than one language?"

Woodgate stood up and stretched his arms toward the sky. "I speak several," he said, seemingly bored.

"What about French? You speak French?"

"Of course," he said.

Caleb reached into the baggy pocket on the side of his fatigues and pulled out a screw of paper. He carefully unfolded the paper and then handed it up to Woodgate. "What do you make of this?"

Woodgate perused the contents with his eyes, his face growing increasingly more serious with each line.

I looked at Caleb, who wore a merry expression as he watched Woodgate read.

"So," said Caleb, as Woodgate reached the bottom of the page and then turned it over to see if there was more on the back, which there was not. "What do you think of that?"

"Where did you find this?" Woodgate asked, accusingly.

"On this island," said Caleb.

"I was with him," I said, sensing a need to corroborate this claim. "We found it in a chamber above the rocks in a place that is a half day's walk down the beach."

"Why don't you read it aloud for Prescott's benefit," said Caleb, who did not speak or read French, but for some reason did not inform Woodgate of this fact.

Woodgate hesitated a moment, glanced at Caleb and me, and then cleared his throat before beginning.

"*Je suis Marguerite*. I am Marguerite," Woodgate smoothly translated, then he again cleared his throat and read more: "*Avant aujourd'hui, je vivais à Paris*. Before today I lived in Paris." Woodgate stopped reading and frowned.

"Don't stop there—it's just getting interesting," encouraged Caleb, smiling.

"Very well," said Woodgate, lifting the paper up to his face and then speaking the following translation: "As a heartbeat is to an eternity, as a teardrop is to the vast sea, as a light breeze is to a hurricane, so am I to the universe—inconsequential, forgotten, and as immaterial as the beam of light that carried me to this island. Oh, but how can this be, when only moments ago I stood beneath the dark umber arch of the Eiffel Tower?"

"Marguerite's a poet," said Caleb, his knees now gathered in his arms. "I bet she'd like to meet me." Caleb turned to me, a wanton grin on his face, his eyebrows twitching for added effect. Then he lifted his right hand and pointed at Woodgate. "Don't stop now, Woody."

Woodgate, at Caleb's prodding, returned to the paper. "She has dated the rest of her entries. This next entry is dated 'April 23, 1998.'" Woodgate shook his head sadly, as I believe it was finally registering with him the magnitude and reality of our unusual situation on the island.

I have produced below, without any interruption to describe the reaction of my island mates, the remainder of Woodgate's translation.

April 23, 1998

I am currently a sojourner on this tropical isle. Found: food, shelter, comfort. Unfound: another living soul, the way home.

April 24, 1998

The walls of this stone chamber, where I now pass long days and longer nights, are scribbled and scratched with names and dates—dates that occur long before my time, and even more disconcerting, long after my time. I look for meaning in all that I see. I watched a monarch butterfly alight upon a stone today, only to be swallowed by the sudden rush of the sea.

April 28, 1998

There is an invisible force pulling at me, drawing me inland. In my dreams I have seen a pretty seaside port where two ships peacefully rise and fall with the tides. Each ship travels to a different location. For some reason, I must choose between the two.

May 3, 1998

I leave this paper behind for posterity, so that some shipwrecked soul may read it and take heart, gain strength in knowing that he is not alone on this strange journey. Today I will leave my roost above the rocks, and then venture inland, where my intuition tells me that I will find inner peace. I arrived here in a flash of light, leaving behind the sadness of a former life, yet I now understand that I must find my way home again, if only to be there for my dear aging mother.

Woodgate leaned down and handed the paper back to Caleb, who gently folded the paper and then returned it to his pocket. None of us spoke for several minutes. Woodgate reached behind his head and rubbed his neck, his eyes on the sand by his feet, but his thoughts faraway. I sat quietly and thought about Marguerite. Did she ever see her mother again? Did she walk along the path that leads to the room with the fountain and the tapestry? Did she walk through that portal?

"I," Woodgate began weakly, and then, when Caleb and I looked up, resumed more resolutely. "I had the very same dream—last night."

"What dream?" I asked.

"The dream about the ships in the port, Prescott," said Woodgate. "The choices."

"Do you mean to say that you dreamed what Marguerite dreamed?" I asked, seeking clarification.

Caleb stood up, and walking past Woodgate, said, "You're not the only one, Woody."

"What do you mean?" said Woodgate, now trailing behind Caleb.

"I mean I've had that dream every night since I've been here, man," said Caleb, picking up his rucksack and slinging it over his shoulder. "It's just the island playing with our minds. It's part of the experience, right, Pres?"

I laughed nervously and nodded, and I purposely chose not to reveal to Caleb and Woodgate that I had never had any such dream since arriving on the island. As a matter of fact, I was too embarrassed to tell them about my most recent dream: I sat in a schoolroom full of children my own age. I looked down at myself to discover to my horror that I wore only my undergarments, which humiliated me greatly. My classmates pointed and laughed at my near nakedness, and then I heard a tap on my desk, and looked up to discover my teacher was a talking penguin.

Chapter Twenty-Two
SEPARATING

THERE WAS A TENSION, an unmistakable tension, after Woodgate read the diary entries by the French woman. Caleb continued to rummage through his rucksack, absentmindedly searching for something he could not seem to find, as if there existed another dimension in that green rectangular bag. Woodgate, clearing his throat constantly, sat upon Caleb's new bench and pulled out his leathern book. I watched him as he read, the spine of the book covering his long nose, but I also noticed that he never once turned the page—perhaps, I thought, there is another dimension in that book and he cannot find the end of the words on that page.

"I'm off," said Caleb, his rucksack slung over his shoulder.

"Where are you going?" I asked.

"I need to get some exercise," said Caleb, shrugging his big shoulders. "I'll be back later." He turned and left. I had expected him to ask me to accompany him, as he usually did, but the invitation never materialized, and for some reason I did not have the courage to ask to come along.

After Caleb disappeared down the hill, Woodgate became suddenly active. He walked over to the hooch and gathered some clothing, placed his book in his shirt pocket, picked off a banana from the bunch that sat out of the sun beneath the canopy of the shelter, and then announced, "I have decided to do some exploring of my own, Prescott."

"Exploring?"

"I shan't be too long." Woodgate slowly disappeared down the hill, listing a little, favoring his right leg.

I moved to edge of the cliff and looked down. I could see Caleb wading through the water, his trousers rolled up to his thighs, his heavy black boots hung by their shoestrings around his neck. He was traveling in the direction of the stone statues, toward the inland path that I had traversed the day before.

Woodgate, I later learned, traveled north, in the direction of the French woman's lair, though did not reach it.

I turned and faced our campsite. The fire smoldered, producing a thin trail of black smoke that rose away from the sea. I untied my black hair ribbon, ran my hands alongside my head, pushing my hair back into a ponytail, and then retied the ribbon. The afternoon sun beamed down, overheating me, so I pulled off my sleeveless waistcoat and then pulled off my white shirt. Peeking over the cliff, I searched for and found Caleb, walking a long way up the beach.

I hastily entered the hooch and searched through some of Caleb's personal effects, my heart booming in my chest. I found his green military vest, with its baggy pockets in the front. The garments seemed engendered with power and manliness, just like Caleb, whereas my white pullover shirt, with its neck and underarm gussets and its chest and wrist ruffles, seemed effeminate in contrast. I dropped my waistcoat and shirt and then picked up Caleb's vest. What would it feel like to wear such a garment? Satisfied that no one was near, I pulled it on. Though it was too big for me, I felt all the more brave with it against my skin. If only there were a looking glass. I walked into the sunlight and marveled at my shadow. I spent several minutes walking around the campsite wearing this vest, occasionally running my hands over the material in admiration. I lifted the flap on the right front pocket and slipped my hand inside and discovered an object. When I drew it out of the pocket, I was surprised to see that it was a medal of some sort, a purple ribbon with a white border attached to a gold heart-shaped medal that had a purple heart inside it. A man's head, shown in profile in raised relief, appeared gold against the purple heart-shaped background. On the flip side it simply read, "For Military Merit: Caleb Thompson."

"I got that for my bad luck," Caleb told me later that day, after I lied that I had found it in the sand by the hooch.

"They present awards in your time for bad luck?" I asked.

Woodgate, whose nose had been buried in the spine of his book, lowered his hands and focused on our conversation.

"They do when you get shot." Caleb picked up the piece of skewered fish he had cooked in the fire and placed in on a palm leaf.

"You were shot? By a gun?" I said, amazed.

Caleb carefully handed me the palm leaf with the cooked fish on it and then stood up. He turned around and began to unbuckle his pants. Curious, Woodgate now leaned in.

"I was with my platoon in a small Vietnamese village, if you want to call it that," he said, looking over his shoulders at us. He lowered his pants and then let them fall to his ankles. It was then that I realized that this was a bit of theater that Caleb had performed before, no doubt for his war comrades back in Vietnam. "The town consisted of three or four huts and a dinky little rice field. We searched each hut for Viet Cong, our enemy. But all we found was a nest of Vietnamese woman clutching their children, cowering in a dark corner of a hut.

"Then bang-bang-bang—a high-caliber rifle in the distance. The platoon scattered, our sergeant shouted commands, and we hunkered down while bullets sprayed around us." Caleb got down on his hands and knees, in a crawling position, his trousers still bunched at his ankles. He looked foolish, and it was very apparent that he relished this fact. "I was moving along like this when—whap!—I thought a king cobra sank his fangs in me." Caleb swiped at the air with his forefinger and middle finger extended to illustrate the fanged mouth of a snake attacking.

"Where?" I asked.

Caleb pulled down his white undergarments and revealed his right buttocks. "Right here—of all places," said Caleb, a huge smile on his face.

"Good God," said Woodgate, squinting his eyes to view the healed wound, which was a reddish scar about the length and thickness of three of my fingers. "That is hideous."

As Caleb rose, pulling up his under shorts and then his military trousers, he said, "Thank you. I'm quite proud of it."

Caleb sat down cross-legged next to me, retrieved his fish, and began eating. "Actually, you should have seen it when I first got shot," said Caleb, as he chewed. "It looked like a butchered hog. I thought it was my ticket out of Nam. I spent about three weeks in the hospital—where I received this Purple Heart Medal—but then they sent me back into the jungle with my platoon." Caleb rubbed the medal with his thumb. "I keep this with me, for conversation purposes." He placed the medal back into his pocket. "It gets me a lot of laughs."

It was getting dark, and as lay there in the sand around the cooking fire, my head resting on my elbow, I naturally associated that time of night with the events that occurred twenty-four hours before, when we buried the unfortunate airplane pilot. As I visualized in my mind the newly dug grave, Woodgate cleared his throat and spoke.

"Are either of you going to ask me how I spent my day?" he said, sitting cross-legged, his book perched on his crossed ankles.

"Should we, Woody?" asked Caleb.

"What is the reason you insist on calling me Woody?" said Woodgate, his eyebrows pressing downward.

"Because I figure you prefer it over 'scarecrow' or 'beanpole,'" said Caleb, that ever-present smile, beaming all the more powerfully.

"You think you're a riot, don't you?" said Woodgate, annoyed.

"What did you do today, Mr. Woodgate?" I asked, desperately resisting the urge to laugh at Caleb's clowning, and eager to avoid giving Caleb an opportunity to create another more insulting nickname for Woodgate.

Woodgate cleared his throat. "Thank you, Prescott, for your old-fashioned manners." He cleared his throat again. "Well, I walked along the southern beach and contemplated our circumstances and searched for some answers."

"Did you?" said Caleb in a sarcastic tone.

"I did," answered Woodgate. "And I concluded that my training, all of my previous life experiences, any of the thousands of books I have read, have not prepared me for this situation. But," Woodgate thrust up his forefinger to emphasize a change in direction, "I have a mathematical mind, a logical mind, and with time and more information I believe I can solve this mystery; furthermore, I believe that the solution will prove to be less extraordinary than we could ever forecast."

"More information, sir?" I said. "What do you mean?"

"Well, simple," Woodgate said, shrugging his shoulders. "You and Caleb are my resources. You've been here longer than I. Tell me everything you know."

"What's there to tell?" said Caleb. "Two months ago I was in Vietnam, in 1968; three weeks ago Prescott was on a ship off the coast of England, in 1779; yesterday you were on a battlefield in France, in 1916, and now we're here, in limbo."

"But, Caleb, what about what happened to me yesterday?" I said.

"Oh yeah." Caleb yawned. "And yesterday, just before I picked your bony butt off of the beach, Prescott went inland, entered a marble portico, and saw Love and Death."

"Love and Death!" Woodgate's back straightened. "Whatever do you mean?"

I then provided Woodgate with a quick summary of my trip inland to the footbridge, the cave, the portico, and great hall.

"You are certain the tapestries read 'Love and Death'"? Woodgate asked.

"Yes, sir. Does it mean anything to you?"

"It may," he said. "Tomorrow, in the sunlight, I have something that I think will be of great interest to you."

"What?" Caleb said.

"Tomorrow, boys," said Woodgate. "I'll show you tomorrow. As for now, I am tired and confused. I did not sleep much last night. Time for bed."

Woodgate rose, walked into the hooch, and then lay down on the palm leaves that I had placed there several weeks earlier. It was clear to me now that I had lost my bed.

"Get your sleep, old sport," said Caleb, mimicking Woodgate's accent. "That way your great logical mind will be razor sharp in the morning when we must choose between eating bananas or kiwi fruit."

"I am going to choose kiwi fruit," I said.

"That is because you cannot break the code of the banana peel the way Woody can," said Caleb in a voice that he purposely projected for Woodgate to hear. Caleb grinned ear-to-ear; obviously very pleased with his cleverness.

Woodgate remained silent, and in moments he was snoring.

Chapter Twenty-Three
MINIATURE MARCHERS

CALEB ROUSED ME FROM MY SLEEP just as the morning sky began to take on a yellowish hue, though the stars still twinkled overhead. "Prescott," he whispered. "Get up. We need to go check something out."

I reacted slowly; sleep still swimming in my brain. "What? What do we need to check?" I ran my hands across my face and rubbed my sleep-encrusted eyes.

"I had a dream," he said, "and I have to see if it plays out."

"Plays out? Whatever do you mean?" The air was cool so I picked up my waistcoat, which I had used as a pillow, and then donned it.

Minutes later we were on the beach below, and I expected Caleb to head south, as we normally did when gathering water and food, but he headed north, toward the statues and where I swam onto this island almost four weeks ago.

By the time we moved beyond the cliffs below our encampment, the stars had receded from view and the sun now rose alongside the volcano at the island's center, barely peeping over the jungle canopies at the edge of the beach.

"Are you going to tell me your dream, Caleb?" I said, struggling to keep up with his long strides.

Caleb, still walking, focused his eyes on me and moved his head up and down in an exaggerated manner. "I think you've grown since you arrived, Pres. You're taller . . ."

"Caleb," I protested. "The dream!"

Caleb threw his head back and laughed heartily.

"OK—the dream. It was so vivid—so real," said Caleb, suddenly grave in his delivery. "I've had so many weird dreams since I arrived on this island, but this one takes the cake." Caleb lifted his arm and pointed ahead. "It should be up there, a little beyond the statues."

"What?" I asked, now a little winded.

"I dreamt that there was a colony of ants, killer African ants, coming out of holes in the ground."

"Killer ants?"

"Yeah. As they came out they immediately formed a line, about ten or twelve ants across, and began marching into the jungle, out of the sunlight on the beach and into the shade."

"And?" I did not see what was so important about ants escaping into the jungle.

"We're almost there," Caleb said. "I'll tell you more in a moment."

"Caleb," I whined as he trotted ahead, at first in a slow jog, then at a running pace. I let him move well ahead of me, watching him run past the stone statues and then onto a flat piece of beach at the edge of the jungle, some two hundred feet past the inland trail that I had followed two days earlier.

I was looking down at the deep indents in the sand where Caleb's big boots had kicked up the sand, when I heard him hooting and hollering. I gazed up to see him standing still, his arms akimbo, oscillating his head as he stared at the ground. "I was right!" he shouted. "Hurry up, Prescott." He turned and beckoned me by waving his hand rapidly above his head.

I freely admit that I was fearful of these killer ants. I had never heard of such an organism and my imagination formed images of giant ants with dagger-like pincers, insects that could jump up and bite me in the face, consume my flesh like a deadly school of piranhas. Nevertheless, I increased my pace from a rapid walk to a medium jog, pumping my arms more than the effort required, which in my mind gave the impression of greater willingness to make an approach.

Caleb stood on a hard packed yellow-brown surface, not loose granular sand like could be found closer to the surf. Reddish ants, each about half the size of my thumb, emerged from a dozen or so holes. It was confusion, chaos, with no discernable pattern, except that the frenzied movement eventually funneled into a twenty-five foot line that marched along briskly into the jungle vegetation. This scene sent me reeling back into the past. On more than three occasions I had witnessed houses in Boston engulfed in flames, and watched as every available volunteer ran to and fro carrying water buckets in an attempt, usually fruitless, to extinguish the blaze. This frantic movement, the choreographed mayhem of my neighbors, seemed synonymous to the ants' desperate attempt to escape the burning sunlight.

Caleb smiled at me, no doubt deeply satisfied that his dream had come to fruition. Then I became curious. Had Caleb seen these ants yesterday when, after listening to Woodgate's translations of the French woman's diary, he walked along this very stretch of beach? Had he created the story of the dream to play a trick on me, to fool me for laughs?

"No, I didn't," Caleb insisted when I broached the subject. "I saw the ants on this very spot in my dream. And a voice spoke to me, narrated the action. It was like one of those nature shows, like 'Mutual of Omaha's Wild Kingdom.' As a matter of fact,"

Caleb snapped his fingers and bit his lower lip. He expression was graver still. "It was Marlin Perkins' voice that I heard."

"Slow down, Caleb. I do not understand."

"OK, OK," said Caleb, taking a breath. "You know about television—the box that carries moving images. We've talked about it a bunch of . . ." (I nodded that I understood) "OK, Marlin Perkins was the host of 'Wild Kingdom,' which was a show I loved and used to watch before I went to Nam. The show was about animals, especially African animals—elephants, lions, giraffes."

"I understand."

"OK—I saw the ants from above entering the jungle in this line, and Marlin Perkins's voice explained the motivation for the ants leaving the beach."

"What was the reason?"

"A tsunami," he said, now staring blankly at the great red line.

"A what?"

"It's a tidal wave, I'm pretty sure," said Caleb, springing to life again. "Marlin Perkins said that Tsunamis are caused by earthquakes or," he pointed to the center of the island, "by volcanic activity."

"A tidal wave? What is that?"

"A giant wave, Prescott. They're deadly when they're big enough."

"And these ant, these killer ants," I said, making sure that I stood well away from the red path, "tell you that there will be a giant wave?"

Caleb leaned down and let an ant climb onto his hand, and then yelled "Ouch!" as he whipped his hand violently in an attempt to throw the insect off. "That little bugger just bit me!"

"You picked it up," I said, laughing. "It's a killer ant, right?"

"Come on," said Caleb, putting his hand behind my back and leading me away.

"Let's not give them any ideas that we might taste good."

Our stiff-legged fast-walk quickly transmuted into a sprint, one that did not end until we reached the spot where I first met Caleb among the poles that he had placed in the sand.

Once in the shade of the cliffs, Caleb dropped to the ground and then rolled onto his back, gasping for air and sweating profusely. I plopped down next to him and mirrored his supine position, also supporting myself by leaning back on my elbows.

It was now an exceptional low tide. Petite waves gently tumbled onto the sand; their feeble efforts unable to obscure a great reef of rocks whose normal existence was among the mermaids in the murky depths. I had never witnessed as much beach in front of the cliffs as showed now.

When our breathing slowed enough to converse, I again asked Caleb to explain the connection between the killer ants and the giant wave that his dream had prophesied.

"Animals can sense changes in the atmosphere that we cannot feel," said Caleb. "Have you ever heard of animals forecasting the weather?"

"I have heard of cows sitting before a rainstorm."

"There you have it," said Caleb. "Those ants may recognize a change in air pressure that we do not sense, and so they move inland to wait out the storm or the tidal wave."

"What about us?" I asked. "Should we hurry up and return to our encampment?"

Caleb searched the sea with his eyes. "The waves look harmless right now. But, I suppose we should play it safe and get back to the hooch."

We stood up and began walking, a little faster than our normal pace but certainly not hurriedly, toward the steep incline that led to the cliff-top encampment.

"Is the hooch high enough? Will it withstand a giant wave?"

"I'd say, Pres, it all really depends on how big that wave is."

Chapter Twenty-Four
INTERPRETING

LYING ON HIS BACK, his arms across his chest, his opossum-like nose pointed toward the underside of the tarp, Woodgate slept peacefully in the hooch.

"He looks like a corpse," joked Caleb, as soon we arrived at our encampment. "Go place a mirror under his nose to see if he's still breathing."

"His chest rises and falls," I said, as I moved into the hooch. "He is no more dead than you or me."

"Comforting," said Caleb, now standing behind me, looking down at the sleeping man.

I knelt down and pushed Woodgate's shoulder, nudged him a little to wake him. "Mr. Woodgate. Time to wake up."

He opened one eye, grimaced, and then said, "What on earth for?"

I looked up at Caleb, hoping he would continue from there, but he did not.

"I was having the most wonderful dream," said Woodgate, now sitting up. "I saw people dancing, women in white gowns and men in formal wear. We were near the water, on a pleasant dock, where two ships gently rocked, their high canvas sails flagging, porters busily carrying cargo and luggage up and down gangplanks."

Caleb and I traded glances.

"Mr. Woodgate," I said. "We think we may be in some danger, from the natural elements."

Woodgate stood up, pulled on his shirt and began buttoning it. "No doubt we are."

"What do you mean, sir?"

"Prescott, about that business we began last night. Do you remember I told you I have something interesting to show you?"

"Of course."

Woodgate moved to a nearby boulder and Caleb and I followed. He withdrew the leathern book from his shirt pocket and then placed it on the stone. "Gentlemen, please examine this."

He flipped through the pages, which were scribbled upon in dark ink, the penmanship spidery, with many instances where words appeared to have been hastily crossed out. Many of the pages had blocks of letters and nonsense words. One such block looked like this:

```
M E D I C
M f z t n i/j
E g l d s b
D y v p e a
I k c u w r
C o m x q h
```

This simple box of letters, Woodgate later explained to me, was based on a Polybius square, an invention by an ancient Greek scholar named Polybius. Co-ordinates in the grid represent each letter in the alphabet. The key is as follows:

A: dc	F: mm	L: ee	Q: ci	V: de
B: ec	G: em	M: ce	R: ic	W: ii
C: ie	H: cc	N: mi	S: ei	X: cd
D: ed	I/J: mc	O: cm	T: md	Y: dm
E: di	K: im	P: dd	U: id	Z: me

The German Army, using a machine called a telegraph, would send a series of dots and dashes known as Morse code along the airwaves to communicate instantly with other German military personnel hundreds of miles away. The telegraph operator could represent every letter in the alphabet using these dots and dashes. The English and French, enemies to the Germans, easily intercepted this invisible information; however, only a few specially trained code-breakers like Woodgate could decipher it.

Woodgate sat in the dirty battlefield trenches systematically working on the ciphers in his leathern book, which accounted for the many crossed out attempts throughout the book. He explained that the "MEDIC" code (above) was a moderately difficult cipher for him to break, and he derived great satisfaction when he succeeded.

The message he deciphered saved many lives because it thwarted a surprise attack. Here is the deciphered message along with the corresponding co-ordinates:

S T R I K E A T D A Y B R E A K
ei md ic mc im ed dc md ed dc dm ec ic di dc im

Woodgate finally settled on a page that looked very much different from the entries before it. Constructed in cursive lettering and organized into neat stanzas was a poem, clearly titled at the top, "Love and Death," and below the title, "Lines composed in 1885 by William Butler Yeats."

Woodgate picked up the book, brought it close to his eyes, and began reading aloud the following: "Behold the flashing waters; a cloven, dancing jet which from the milk-white marble forever foam and fret." Woodgate looked up. "Sound familiar?"

"What is this some kind of a joke?" Caleb said. "Did you write that little poem while we were gone?"

"No, Caleb, I did not. I only wish I could construct lines of this caliber."

"Please continue," I urged, chills running like African ants down my spine.

"I will, Prescott," Woodgate said. "But first, do you recall seeing a marble fountain with a cloven jet?"

"Yes—definitely!"

"Very good," said Woodgate. He shut the book and placed it back in his pocket.

"What are you doing?" Caleb shouted.

"I shan't read anymore until I know more." Woodgate tapped his temple with his index finger.

Caleb moved to within an inch of Woodgate, and with as fierce a look as I have ever seen him make, spoke in a slow rasp through gritted teeth. "You are going to take that book out of your pocket right now, Woodgate, or I am going to come and get it."

"You do not understand . . ."

"GIVE IT!" Caleb shouted, grabbing Woodgate's shirt.

"Unhand me, you savage!" Woodgate implored, as he tried to wiggle out of Caleb's grip. Woodgate's effete resistance was no match for Caleb, however; in two precise and lightning fast moves, Caleb upended Woodgate and threw him to the sand. This grappling technique was executed on Caleb's part with next to no effort, which I am certain registered plainly to Woodgate. One did not have to possess the mathematical mind of a code-breaker to realize that Woodgate was powerless against Caleb's brawn and athleticism.

Caleb moved in front of Woodgate, lightly kicked at the sole of one of Woodgate's boots, held his hand out, then calmly said, "Take it out of your pocket and hand it over."

I backed up a few steps, fearful that tempers would flare further and one of these giant men would fall upon me.

"You Americans are such bullies," said Woodgate as he reached for his pocket.

"You British are such control freaks," retorted Caleb.

Woodgate handed the leathern book over to Caleb, who then walked several steps away and began flipping through the book.

"If you had simply given me a little time, I was going to read the rest," said Woodgate, getting up and brushing sand from the seat of his trousers. "I simply wanted to hear more details of Prescott's journey inland."

"Whatever for?" Caleb said, as he searched the pages of the book.

"The human mind has a way of attaching suggestions to memories," said Woodgate. "If I had read the poem in its entirety, Prescott likely would have interpreted it as being solely about what he saw. It is called the power of suggestion."

"So?" Caleb had found the page with the poem, and his eyes were quickly scanning it, his lips moving rapidly as he read.

Woodgate raised his chin in the air, placed his hands at his side, retreated to Caleb's bench, and then sat down.

"What does it say, Caleb?" I asked.

"Behold the flashing waters;/A cloven dancing jet,/That from the milk-white marble/For ever foam and fret;/Far off in drowsy valleys/Where the meadow saffrons blow,/The feet of summer dabble/In their coiling calm and slow./The banks are worn forever/By a people sadly gay:/A Titan with loud laughter,/Made them of fire clay./Go ask the springing flowers,/And the flowing air above,/What are the twin-born waters,/And they'll answer Death and Love."

Caleb's voice trailed off at the end, and then he looked at me sadly.

I privately conjectured that the author of this poem was once a citizen on this island, during the 1800s; and therefore the inspiration for the poem came from looking upon the creations—the cave, the great hall, and the footbridge—that the poet's contemporaries had created.

"What do you make of it, Caleb?"

"I don't know, Prescott. I don't know."

"Perhaps I can say a few words? It is my book, and I am the most familiar with the poem," said Woodgate, his legs crossed, his voice haughtier than ever.

Caleb and I turned our eyes to Woodgate.

"Very good," said Woodgate, standing up and then pacing back and forth in front of the bench, his hands clasped behind his back. "In the Yeats poem, the narrator writes of a 'Titan with loud laughter made out of fire and clay.' I believe . . ."

"The volcano!" interrupted Caleb.

"Exactly my thought!" said Woodgate. "The volcano is made of fire and clay and its loud laughter would be . . ."

"An eruption!" Caleb said.

"Or the rumbling sounds it makes," Woodgate said.

"We heard rumblings two days ago, just before you arrived," I said.

"Is that so?" said Woodgate. "Then I am sure it will do so again."

I looked up at the great volcano jutting out of the center of the verdant isle; the black chimney-like smoke puffed out of its conical apex and chugged eastward, eventually disappearing above the low-lying, fair-weather clouds.

"That thing could blow at any moment," said Caleb.

"And, of course, if it does, we have no chance," said Woodgate, pacing anew. "Now, Yeats writes that the twin-born fountains are named 'Death and Love' in the first stanza. However, the second stanza refers to Love and Death as spirits."

"Second stanza," I said, confused.

"Caleb has not read the second stanza yet," said Woodgate. "Why don't you do so, Caleb?"

Caleb looked down at the text and read the following: "With wreaths of withered flowers/Two lonely spirits wait,/With wreaths of withered flowers/'Fore paradise's gate./They may not pass the portal/Poor earth-enkindled pair,/Though sad is many a spirit/To pass and leave them there."

"Stop there!" commanded Woodgate. "Last night Prescott spoke of a door, a portal, in that great hall. He spoke of the tapestries with the words love and death embroidered upon them. Prescott, did any of those tapestries depict withered flowers?"

"Yes, sir. They did"

"Can those spirits pass through that portal? No, of course not," said Woodgate, pacing ever faster, his voice rising in pitch. "But I suppose some sad spirits—the French woman, perhaps—have passed and left them there."

Caleb looked over at me, and I am sure he read the wide-eyed expression on my face as being similar to someone who has seen a ghost.

"The last two lines of the poem are important, in my view," said Woodgate. "As a code-breaker, all clues must fit exactly or it's all hogwash. So, Prescott, I put this to you: What do the lines, 'By the door of Mary's garden/Are the spirits Love and Death,' mean to you?"

"What do you mean?"

"You saw the tapestries labeled Love and Death. But did you see any spirits?"

"No, sir, but I did hear a spirit's voice."

"Very well, but did you see a garden?"

"I did not," I said.

"Woodgate," said Caleb, in a confident voice. "Who's to say that the garden is not beyond the door, beyond the portal? And if this poem truly relates to us and this island, then who's to say that the portal is not paradise's gate?"

"What do you mean by paradise's gate, Caleb," I asked.

Caleb looked down at the book. "The poem states that these two spirits with the withered flowers forever wait before paradise's gate. Paradise's gate! To me this must mean Heaven."

"And Mary is the mother of God," I said.

"And her garden is beyond that portal," Caleb said, finishing my very thoughts.

"Gentlemen! Gentlemen! Please, let's not put the cart before the horse." Woodgate looked down his nose at the two of us. "We know nothing until we prove otherwise."

"Prove otherwise?" Caleb threw the book at Woodgate, who showed remarkable dexterity by catching it in his left hand without even watching its arc in flight. The whole time, Woodgate's eyes never left Caleb's. "How do we prove otherwise, Woodgate?"

"Simple," said Woodgate, placing the book back into his shirt pocket and then standing up straight. "We open that door."

Chapter Twenty-Five
DILLY-DALLYING

"DO YOU KNOW WHAT A TSUNAMI IS?" Caleb asked Woodgate, suddenly changing the subject, although I understood the reason for this abrupt transition.

"It is a Japanese word," said Woodgate, who then walked a few steps to the hooch and gathered his greatcoat, military hat, which I'd never seen him wear, and a leathern belt with bulky square pouches attached to it. Then ducking from under the tarp and stepping back out into the sunlight, Woodgate said, "Tsu means harbor and Nami means wave—a wave in the harbor, I suppose, is the best translation I can come up with at the moment."

"You also speak Japanese, sir?" I asked, amazed.

"Actually," Caleb said. "A tsunami is more than a wave in the harbor, at least in modern terms. It is a tidal wave—a giant, very destructive wave that crashes onto land."

"Fascinating," said Woodgate, sarcastically.

"Sir, this very morning Caleb brought me to see ants scurrying away from the beach into the jungle," I said.

"Really? Well, I saw a birdie flying above the volcano." Woodgate, obviously being sarcastic, put on his high, wide-brimmed hat, which made him several inches taller and appear several times skinnier.

"I'd like to drop you into that volcano," said Caleb under his breath, but loud enough for Woodgate to hear.

"No need to, because that is where I am going. I'd recommend you accompany me if you want to go home."

"You're going to open that portal, huh?" said Caleb.

"I am. You should come along, if you want to go home."

Caleb rubbed the back of his neck and grimaced. "If you had asked me this question last night, I would have said no—absolutely not. But this morning I had a dream about ants on the beach—down by the statues—and, while you slept, Prescott and I visited the spot

117

where my dream took place, and there were the ants, scurrying into the jungle, just like in my dream."

"What—"

Caleb raised his hand and exposed his palm to Woodgate. "Wait! Don't say another word. Let me speak—let me finish, for God's sake!"

"Very well—speak."

"Thank you. I will." Caleb quickly summarized the particulars of his dream as they related to forecasting the tsunami. He then explained that volcanic activity and earthquakes could cause mountainous waves to suddenly appear. Woodgate listened without interrupting, but the torpid look on his face indicated that he was not moved by the information.

"The French woman wrote of dreams that implored her to move inland." Woodgate walked to the edge of the cliff as he spoke and looked down at the sea. "I have had such dreams, every night—as we all have."

It was another opportunity for me to admit that the island did not talk to me in my sleep. Inexplicably, I held my tongue.

"What are you implying?" Caleb asked.

Woodgate turned and lifted his arms from his sides. "I am not implying anything. I have stated moments before and I state again: we must go open that door—that portal."

"To what—enter Mary's garden?"

"Yes. That or to find a way home or . . . Do you want to spend the rest of your life living atop of a cliff like animals?"

Caleb did not answer this question; instead, he entered the hooch and began gathering his belongings, consisting of several articles of clothing that he stuffed into his rucksack, and the long green-handled knife, which he placed in the leathern sheath attached to his trouser belt.

"Do you want to go home?" Woodgate asked me in a low voice.

The thought processes that this question instigated within my mind intrigued me, as the answer to the question should have been easy to say, but instead lodged in my throat and stayed there. I knew I should want to go home, to that concept of home, but I did not know where to call my home, which muddied the waters. I had very little connection to Boston, because, though my brother resided there, he was but a stranger to me. What did returning home mean, anyway? Was it Boston? Was it the *Bonhomme Richard*? I did not think I wanted to return to the war—a war that had long ago been decided.

"I cannot easily say," I mumbled.

"What about your family and loved ones?" Woodgate asked, his voice tinged with sadness.

"I do not have anybody to return to," I said. "My parents are dead. I have only a brother, and that in name only. He cares little for me. And, to be honest, I have seen the future, through you and Caleb, and it makes the past appear . . ." The word to finish this thought would not avail itself to me.

"Insignificant?" offered Woodgate.

"How can I go back?" I said. "I know of trains and planes and world wars and scientific discoveries a hundred years off. I know of electricity and machines that make music. I would be considered a lunatic."

"What if passing through that portal brings us somewhere more sublime than home? The poem referred to it as paradise's gate."

"Do you mean Heaven?" This question unnerved me. After all, entering Heaven is the same as passing into death.

"I suppose a giant wave could land on us here and sweep us out to sea," said Woodgate. "Or the volcano could erupt and reduce us to ashes. Or a poisonous snake could slither out of the bushes one night and bite you. Or you could eat something that . . ."

"We get the point, Woodgate," said Caleb, emerging from the hooch.

"My point is that the outcome would be the same. But what if there is more beyond that portal? What if it does lead us back? We are supposed to move inland—to open that door."

"What if we don't like what we see when we open it?" Caleb asked.

"Each man decides his own fate—pass through the portal or not."

"You'll come with us, won't you?" Caleb said to me. "At least as far as the portal?"

"You are going?" I said, somewhat surprised.

Caleb nodded his head. "I want to see what's on the other side. You'll come too, right?"

I began to cry.

Caleb walked alongside and gently squeezed the back of my neck with his hand, and then he patted me on the back several times. "If we leave you behind, you're on your own. I won't be here to protect you anymore. But if you come with us and don't like what you see beyond that door—heck, if we all don't like what we see—we can all turn back."

"You're only a child, Prescott," said Woodgate. "You cannot stay here alone."

"With all due respect, sir," I said, badly masking my irritation. "I believe you underestimate me. I am not a child. I will turn thirteen in a matter of . . .." How could I finish this statement when I did not know the day or by what calendar my life was being navigated?

"Prescott, my man, look at me," said Caleb in a soothing voice. I peered up at him, my eyes blurry with tears. "Will you come with us?"

"As far as the portal—yes," I said, sniffling and wiping my eyes with my sleeve; a poor attempt to gain composure. "Into eternity—I don't know."

Chapter Twenty-Six
RUMBLE IN THE JUNGLE

ONE SUMMER DAY'S END, some time ago, I ran an errand for my brother that carried me down Milk Street to the bustling Boston wharfs. As the day was dying, the ale-colored sunlight poured over everything—the cobblestone lanes, the tallow-colored sails, the rough-hewn granite buildings, the distant church spires—and though this was a district abuzz with commerce (wooden crates and boxes stacked higgledy-piggledy, sailors climbing the masts and spars of the docked ships, boys my age carrying wares up and down gangplanks, and artisans standing behind carts piled high with items for sale), I stumbled upon a game that employed my mind and wasted my time for the better part of an hour.

My objective had been to visit the chandler whose small shop looked onto Long Wharf. There I was to purchase a crate of candles and carry them back to my brother's house in time for an evening meeting he had arranged with an important local merchant whose business my brother coveted. But, I soon got sidetracked when I turned down a narrow alley that was a shortcut to the chandler, and became a spectator of what I learned was called the thimblerig game.

A large man, made more of meat than of bone, who was short in stature but rounder at the waist than a wagon wheel, sat on a box with a board placed upon his lap. The man kept three thimbles on the wooden board that he balanced on his thighs and played at hiding a pea beneath one of the thimbles. The man first revealed under which thimble he placed the pea, and then he quickly moved the thimbles to and fro and round and round with fascinating and dizzying dexterity. A wealthy merchant, in powdered wig and brass-buttoned waistcoat, stood watching the moving thimbles with the concentration of a cat following the flight of a moth, and after wagering a shilling, pointed to a thimble that he believed hid the pea; but, when the thimble-rigger lifted the thimble, it was empty of the pea. A correct guess would have doubled the merchant's money; however, this time, he guessed wrong and forfeited his coin. I wanted to clap my hands in appreciation and joy, but common sense told me that it would be impolite, and I did not want to draw attention to myself and therefore be asked to leave.

I climbed into the low branches of a small elm tree that seemed to grow from the foundation of a building, and watched time and time again as the thimble-rigger drummed up business. "It won't cost but a mere shilling, sir, to play my little game," said the thimble-rigger to each merchant who ventured past him. "Many a man has doubled his money for making a correct guess."

My perch afforded a bird's eye view of the game, and, because I could see the thimble-rigger from the side and above, I very soon realized that he cheated, by way of sleight of hand. On the occasion when a merchant had guessed correctly, the thimble-rigger adroitly removed the pea as he lifted the thimble. It was deception and artifice, which astonished and excited me, though it should have appalled me.

Time has a funny way of slipping away when you are thus entertained, and I suddenly looked up and noticed the early twilight sky had given way to greater darkness—I could no longer make out the pointed tips of the sails in the distance. Without enough light to operate, the thimble-rigger swiftly gathered his effects and, with the board under his arm, passed in front of me. I peered down at him, holding my breath, eager for him to pass without notice of me, but he stopped, looked up, and then reached up his hand. "Here," he said, in a rough voice. "Take this small token in exchange for your silence." He placed two pence in my hand.

"Thank you, sir," I said.

"Speak not a word of my little industry," he said, as he ambled away, "and I will not have to cut out your tongue." He then laughed hoarsely, a laugh that culminated in a sepulchral cough and loud hawking, which doubtless produced a formidable expectoration of phlegm.

I jumped from the tree, making haste to the chandler's shop, but when I arrived the door was closed and the proprietor gone for the evening.

I received a sound beating, later, when I returned to my brother's house empty-handed, and as I lay in my bed that night, I cursed time's slippery ways.

"Time's slippery ways," I said to myself, now looking at the sun above the island and determining that noontime was near. Caleb and Woodgate talked quietly in the hooch while gathering necessities for the journey inland. I blinked my eyes several times and wondered why my mind had ventured into the past, and why, in particular, it dwelled upon that day on the wharfs of Boston. Was there something from that daydream to be learned and then applied to my situation on the island? Was the island talking to me the way it talked to Caleb and Woodgate? No, I decided, it was simply an innocent daydream. But I also understood that time was slippery on this island, a place where it was easy to feel like a pawn, a sheep, or a marionette.

Woodgate walked out of the hooch, shook a couple of canteens that he held in his hands, and said, "I shall return." From this I gathered that he was going to the spring to fill the canteens with water.

It took several minutes, but I managed to work up the courage to approach Caleb to speak what was on my mind. I walked into the hooch, where Caleb was fastening the straps on his rucksack. "I do not trust that man," I blurted out. "He may be luring us into danger?"

"Woodgate?"

"Yes, how can we be sure that he was not sent to retrieve us—playing the thimble game with us and making us expect a pea behind that door?"

"Thimble game? Who's peeing behind a door?" Caleb shook his head in confusion.

"It is a game of deceit that . . ."

"I picked him out of the sand, Pres," said Caleb, interrupting me. "He was unconscious. Nobody is that good an actor."

"You do not find it strange that in two days he has convinced us to leave our encampment here? To go where you once feared to go?"

"I wasn't afraid," Caleb qualified. "I just had . . . I don't know? Feelings."

"These feelings are now gone?"

"We can't stay on the cliff for the rest of our lives." Caleb placed his hand on my upper arm. "I promise I'll keep an eye on him." Caleb rose to his feet. "Here he comes." Caleb nodded toward the path, and a moment later Woodgate appeared over the hill. "He's a big bore and a know-it-all, Pres. But I think he's basically harmless."

"Hey, Woody!" Caleb suddenly shouted. "You ready? Or do you need a warm bottle and a nap first?"

"I'm not keeping anyone."

"Let's hit the road, then, gentlemen."

Butterflies fluttered violently in my stomach. I felt like yawning, though I was well rested. I realized then that these two giants from another time had chosen my destiny for me, and it was frustrating. What could I do? To remain behind posed as much danger, in my mind, as going on, especially because I depended on Caleb's physical abilities to live comfortably on the plateau. Without him around, life would not be as carefree and pleasant.

As a rational person, I did not want to believe that I could walk through some magical portal and be spirited back to my own time period—to 1779. But, I also knew that much that occurred on this island was unexplainable and irrational. And since there was little rhyme or reason to how I came to be here, I knew that another illogical means could be used to release me.

"I have some ideas about what might happen to us if we try to go through that door," I said, after some thought.

"Can you talk and walk at the same time?" Woodgate said. His sarcastic and aristocratic tone reminded me of what I disliked about many Englishmen.

"I can," I said, disguising my frustration with this man who, in forty-eight hours, had upset the balance of my life on the island.

Caleb and I had a routine. We each had our specialties, whether it was gathering food, hunting, or cooking. And we shared an equal status and respected each other's opinions. But all had changed, and it seemed as though we were employed in chasing Woodgate's fancies and whims.

Woodgate looked at his wristwatch, which I realized was the one Caleb had pulled off of the dead man who had washed ashore. I would have wagered 100 pounds that he would never wear it—and I would have lost! "How long till we reach the jungle path?"

"Twenty minutes, if we step on it," said Caleb, using an idiomatic phrase that I had never before heard, but that I could understand.

I quickly gathered my coat, jumped into my leather shoes, and followed the men. The relentless sun beamed down on us, and Woodgate was sweating profusely by the time we reached the beach. I wondered if he had any misgivings about traveling at that time of day. Walking in sand is difficult work for the legs, but Caleb and I were used to it; Woodgate, clearly was not. His red face, the constant puffing, the slumping of the shoulders all indicated to me that he was either unused to the tropical heat or in poor physical conditioning—or both.

At one point, as we were only minutes from the shade of the cliffs, Woodgate tripped somehow and fell face-forward into the sand. Caleb and I erupted in laughter, especially when Woodgate, in his rush to rise from the sand, fell again and then rolled over on his back. It was very dramatic.

"I think I am going to die," he said in a whispery voice.

"You're wearing your entire uniform, dummy," said Caleb, standing over him. "Take something off and you won't roast."

Woodgate held out his hand to Caleb. "Give a mule a boost, good man."

Caleb reached down, grasped Woodgate's outstretched hand, and then effortlessly pulled him into a standing position.

"I am overdressed for this occasion," Woodgate said. "Forgive me, gentlemen, but I must do this."

Woodgate unbuttoned his trousers and let them fall to the sand, revealing his scrawny, bowed white legs and blue underwear. He stepped out of his trousers, picked them up, and announced, "I could wring a gallon of sweat out of these." He removed his military jacket and tied the arms of it around his neck. He then tied his trousers around his neck, and then began walking.

Caleb and I, unable to desist, chuckled softly at first, but then laughed with wild abandon—we nearly fell over ourselves as we clapped our hands and slapped our thighs. Woodgate, realizing he was the object of our laughter, looked back and said, "Laugh all you want, men. Enjoy yourselves at my expense." Despite his tone, I saw a sparkle of joy in his eyes.

A short respite in the shade beneath the craggy cliffs, a few quick gulps from the canteen, and then we again forged on. I remember, as the cliffs receded behind us, looking back and gazing up at our encampment. From that angle I could discern the blue tarpaulin of our hooch. I wondered if I would ever again see our island home.

When we reached the entrance to the jungle path, Caleb knocked his fist on the head of one of the statues.

"Good God!" said Woodgate, who had never seen the statues in person; he had only heard my description of them when I had suggested they were somehow related to the tapestries in the great hall. He leaned closer to a statue and began a thorough examination. He drew his hand over the statue's shape, and then stepped back and looked at it from a distance.

"I have some knowledge about sculpture," Woodgate said, "and from what I can tell, this is a mutt."

Caleb looked at Woodgate with a raised eyebrow.

"A mutt?" I said.

"A mongrel," Woodgate said. "An amalgamation of styles and cultures."

"How so?" I asked.

"The rounded bellies," Woodgate said, pointing to the distended abdomens on each likeness, "are Japanese or Indian. It reminds me of Buddha. The feet, turned to the side in a very uncomfortable position, are Egyptian. The hair, curled in the front, but like a helmet elsewhere, is Greek or Roman."

"How old are they?" asked Caleb.

"Impossible to tell," said Woodgate. "They are weathered, faded here and there, but that could occur in a few years' time."

"Death and Love?" I said.

"Yes," said Woodgate in a hesitant voice. "Yes."

We fished through the whirling vines and then entered the hard-packed dirt path. The hissing of the surf, the bright, burning sun, and the whisperings of the sea breezes disappeared behind the vines. All was quiet—too quiet. I was not the only person to feel this way.

"This place gives me the creeps." As soon as Caleb uttered these words, the ground began to rumble, as if a herd of cattle were running past us. I heard an explosion in the distance as the ground now shook violently.

We all fell to our knees, amid the rumbling, and covered our heads to avoid being knocked unconscious by the debris—branches, cocoanuts, and acorn-sized seeds—that fell from the canopies.

Chapter Twenty-Seven
STICKS AND BIRTH STONES

THE RUMBLING LASTED ABOUT 30 SECONDS. I looked up and saw that Caleb and Woodgate were not hurt, and then rose to my feet.

"Caleb," said Woodgate. "You are banned from speaking again."

This comment, its aim to be comical, did not receive any laughs.

"Maybe, Woodgate, if you'd put your pants back on, we wouldn't upset the gods," said Caleb. "You look like a fool."

Caleb and I laughed as Woodgate slowly stepped into his trousers and then hiked them up to his waist.

"Was that what I thought it was?" I asked.

"Bony white bird legs?" Caleb joked.

I laughed uproariously. "No," I said, recovering for a moment. But when I looked at Woodgate, who was still buckling his belt, I laughed anew, which caused Caleb to laugh even louder—a high-pitched chuckle that sounded maniacal.

"All right, all right," Woodgate said, now facing us. "You two have been out here too long if all you can talk about is my legs. And, Prescott, to answer your question—yes, that was what you thought it was: an earthquake caused by volcanic activity. God be with us."

Suddenly composed, Caleb rushed over to the vinery at the edge of the beach and peeked through. "The sea looks calm," he said. "I half expected a tidal wave, although one could be coming. I say we quick-step it to higher ground."

There was much debris on the path, but we managed to walk over or around it. We maintained a vigorous pace, and so none of us spoke for nearly a quarter mile. Then, as we neared the turn that would provide us a view of the footbridge, Caleb, who was in the lead, shot up his right hand.

"The stone!" he said, and then he jogged away from the trail into the knee-high green vegetation consisting mostly of ferns.

Caleb climbed a small incline, which led to a large stone with a flat tabletop surface. We followed him away from the trail and watched as he climbed atop of the stone.

"This is where it all began," Caleb said with joy in his voice. "This is where I found myself when I arrived on this island."

"Really?" said Woodgate. "You never said so before."

Caleb quickly explained to Woodgate about the incidents leading up to his appearance on the stone. As Caleb spoke, Woodgate and I climbed up and onto the stone. Caleb lay on his back to illustrate what he looked like when he suddenly arrived on the island a couple of months before.

"The sun light came in through those branches up there," said Caleb, pointing upward, toward an opening in the canopy of trees.

"You believe you were shot in the back?" asked Woodgate.

"I know I was shot," said Caleb. "I was lying in my own blood."

"But your wound was gone when you appeared here?" Woodgate said.

"Yes."

"What about you, Mr. Woodgate?" I said. "Where were you before you came here?"

"Where was I?" he said. "I'll tell you what—let's take out something to eat and something to drink, and I will regale you with my little story."

Chapter Twenty-Eight
WOODGATE'S STORY

"TO START, GENTLEMEN, I WAS BORN, RAISED, AND EDUCATED entirely in the 'City of Dreaming Spires'—Oxford, England, if you are not familiar with the Matthew Arnold quotation." Woodgate sat with his legs hanging over the edge of Caleb's birthstone, his eyes concentrating on the tangled vegetation in front of him. In the ten minutes that he told his story, he also managed to consume three unripe bananas.

"I never met my father. He was shipped off to fight the Boer War while my mother carried me in her womb; he returned to England in a coffin before I learned to walk. I have seen over-exposed photographs of him—all flash, very little flesh—but it is clear that I am the spitting image of him."

"Your dad was ugly too, huh?" said Caleb impassively, his eyes closed but his lips spread in a smile.

"He—very funny!" Woodgate's eyes darted toward Caleb, then he shook his head in disgust; but I clearly made out a suppressed smile.

"I grew up without a father figure—it was just my mother and me. I had uncles and older male cousins, but none who lived close enough to influence and guide me. So what does a boy—an inquisitive, an intelligent boy—do to fill the gap?"

"You buy some cement or wood putty?"

"Not that kind of a gap!" said Woodgate, who then, upon realizing Caleb was jesting, threw a green banana peel at him, narrowly missing his head. "You are tiresome."

Caleb's comments were hilarious to me, but I managed to refrain from laughing, mostly to avoid seeming disrespectful. I admired Caleb's irreverence, but my strict upbringing would not allow me to emulate it. Therefore, I redirected Woodgate back to the gap he spoke of, though I am quite certain I wore a grin on my face.

"Yes, I filled the gap by communicating with men—great men—from the past. Writers—great thinkers like Emerson, Carlisle, Thoreau, and Immanuel Kant. Philosophers: men of high-minded ideas and ideals. When you read a book, it is a delayed conversation between you and the writer—a sort of time travel.

"A college friend of mine once argued with me on this last point. 'A conversation must be two-sided,' he insisted to me. And I stated that he was assuming that I do not talk back to the text.

"'You cannot talk back to a text,' he told me. But I disagreed. These books, these authors, they were all my friends. 'All dead men,' he told me. And I said, 'Then, I plead guilty to enjoying the company of men who are dead.'"

A resounding silence followed Woodgate's last statement. No doubt, we all contemplated our unique circumstances on this island.

"I attended a reading by an Irish poet named William Butler Yeats," said Woodgate. "He didn't read 'Love and Death' on that occasion, but his words moved me greatly. I was fourteen years old. I was in love with Dorothy Turner—the daughter of a druggist. I then began writing poems of my own—doggerel, really—about unrequited love. Dorothy was my muse."

As Woodgate's story diverged and diverged again, Caleb grew restless. He rolled his eyes. "Less poetry; more about how you came to this island."

"Poetry is my life blood," said Woodgate, reaching into his pocket and retrieving the leathern book. "One particular poem, 'A Psalm of Life,' by the American, Henry Wadsworth Longfellow...."

"I know that poem!" said Caleb, sitting up suddenly. "From high school English."

"Do you?"

"We all had to read it, but I think I complained the most, until something weird happened."

"What?"

"The poem spoke to me."

Once again, I was in the darkness of the past.

Woodgate stood up tall on the stone near Caleb's feet. He closed his eyes and spread out his hands.

"Tell me not in mournful numbers that life is but an empty dream. For the soul is dead that slumbers and things are not what they seem."

Caleb smiled and nodded his head. "Yeah, man. Right on." He seemed in a trance, then his smile extinguished, as if a disturbing thought transfixed him.

"What's wrong?" I asked.

"Say that again!" Caleb demanded.

Woodgate, stepping down from the stone to the ground, again recited the lines, but without the pomp. "Tell me not in mournful numbers that life is but a dream."

"Wait!" said Caleb. "Am I right in interpreting that as meaning that the poet does not want to be told, in a song or a poem, that life is a dream?"

"That's a fair interpretation," said Woodgate.

"Continue," said Caleb.

"All right," said Woodgate. "For the soul is dead that slumbers, and things are not what they seem."

"The soul is dead that slumbers!" interrupted Caleb. "Did you hear that, Prescott?"

I nodded my head.

"Well, what does it mean to you?"

To understand how I felt at that moment, you must consider that I was standing in a timeless jungle analyzing poetry written a hundred years after my birth, with two men who were born two centuries after me. "It seems to me that the poet is saying that one should not sleep through life. I suppose if your soul is asleep," I grew more confident when I noticed Woodgate nodding as I spoke, "you are as good as dead."

"Are we asleep?" interjected Caleb.

"No," I said.

"Then we can't be dead, right?" said Caleb.

"You are taking liberties with the poem, are you not?" Woodgate said. "You are asserting that the poem was written to address our singular experience here on this island."

"You made the same assumption with your 'Love and Death' poem," said Caleb.

"Yes," said Woodgate. "But that was only after Prescott told me about the statues, the tapestries, the fountains. You are doing what I was fearful of doing: using a shoehorn to make the poem fit your situation."

"All right," said Caleb. "But . . ."

"Mr. Woodgate," I interrupted, as Caleb lay back down on the stone surface. "Your story. Will you please continue?"

"Very well," said Woodgate. "I was a very strong student, in all subjects, but especially in mathematics and languages. These unusual academic abilities allowed me to begin at university soon before my sixteenth birthday. It's long story—too long to tell right now. But suffice it to say that my language and mathematics skills were keys to joining in the war effort. I trained for six months with other code breakers, and then the Royal Army shipped me out."

Woodgate leaned against the stone. "I found myself in France sitting in a dog-toothed trench system, covered in fleas and lice, freezing cold, miserable, tired, half-crazy—you name an emotion and I experienced it."

Woodgate stopped speaking. I watched his face, the way his eyes shifted back and forth, up and down, and the way he bit down on and then released the bite on his lower lip. I knew images and memories flew across his mental canvas.

Caleb, now lying with his eyes closed, drummed his fingers on his chest.

"Three days ago," continued Woodgate, in an especially grave voice. "I was in a trench squatting next to my seventeen-year-old mate who had been gunned down soon after being commanded to make a run toward the German trenches.

"I was talking into a Marconi 1 ½ kilowatt set when I heard a great explosion, saw a flash of blinding light, felt the air leave my lungs, felt my legs disappear beneath me, and . . ."

"And what?" said Caleb, opening one eye to look at Woodgate.

Woodgate shrugged his shoulders, closing his eyes as he did.

"You woke up on this island," I said, finishing the story for Woodgate.

"Well, as crazy as it sounds . . . yes."

Caleb sprang up, jumped from the stone, and stood next to Woodgate.

"You got one part wrong," Caleb murmured.

"What?"

"The part where I picked your sorry butt off the beach." Caleb chuckled, patted the grim-faced Woodgate on the buttocks, and then said, "Come on, guys. Let's make tracks."

"Wait, Caleb," I said. "I have a couple of questions for Mr. Woodgate."

Woodgate turned to me.

"What do you believe, sir, happened that brought you here?"

"I . . . I'm not sure," he said.

"Guys," said Caleb, returning the twenty feet that he had walked away from us. "Of course he knows what happened. Don't you, Woody?"

Woodgate remained silent and still.

"You were hit by a grenade or a bomb or a missile—pick your weapon—and you exploded into a million pieces." Caleb made several sound effects with his mouth to mimic a bomb going off, while moving his hands quickly apart to illustrate an explosion.

"Let me put this in the simplest terms possible, good man," said Caleb, in a poor imitation of a British accent. "I'm dead." Caleb nodded toward me. "Prescott's dead—and you, Woody, I think you were dead when you were alive!"

Once again, Caleb was the only person laughing.

Chapter Twenty-Nine
BACK ON THE TRAIL

IN A MATTER OF MINUTES, we were all standing in front of the footbridge. Caleb's mirth over our apparent demise had reduced from loud hilarity to giddiness, fraught with an almost demented silliness. Caleb suddenly found humor in everything his senses perceived. He had tried, unsuccessfully, to hold in his laughter, but it eventually came bursting out of his nose with a snorting sound. Woodgate censured him several times, but each rebuke stirred in Caleb more hilarity. I would have questioned Caleb's sobriety if I did not know any better: he listed to one side as he giggled, his great black boots pounding the hard-packed trail. At one point, when Woodgate called him a "irksome American," Caleb spat out the water he had drunk and had spittle dripping from his chin. This, of course, was the source of more amusement for Caleb.

Caleb's joviality was, in a small way, a welcomed diversion. Put into perspective, we were walking down a jungle path toward what we believed was a door that opened to eternity. Though I stated earlier that I would not enter the door, I could not say that now. The closer I got to the cave, the more curious I became. The circumstances would dictate my decision. If all seemed well, I would enter. If I sensed danger, I would return to the plateau.

Before we had embarked on this short journey, the men promised me an opportunity to express my ideas about the portal in the great hall. As a matter of fact, Woodgate had sarcastically asked me whether I could talk and walk at the same time. I should have answered "no" to that question, because I had said nothing about that subject since. The earthquake, Caleb's birthstone, Woodgate's circuitous story, and Caleb's temporary madness had precluded me from any opportunity to speak on the subject of the portal. Was this by design? Was Caleb afraid of what I might say?

The footbridge showed no signs of damage as a result of the earthquake. The railing and footboards of the bridge were straight and smooth. No debris cluttered the walkway. Large green leaves hung silently over the bridge's entrance—no monkeys in sight, thankfully. Through the foliage, I could see pieces of the great volcanic mountain.

Something, I'm sure, in the craggy appearance of that great mount, and in the patient puffing of black smoke from its pointed peak, engendered in us all, including Caleb, a sudden solemnity. The volcano was real—a living, breathing dragon in our minds—and was closer than ever. So close, in fact, that Caleb reached out his hand and said, "It seems as though, if I stretched a little more, I could touch it."

"Well, Caleb," said Woodgate, "I don't know about that, but I do know that if the volcano so desired, it could easily reach you."

I was the first to step onto the footbridge. As I walked I sensed the eyes of my companions watching me, and then there was a collective sigh when the bridge supported my weight and nothing cataclysmic occurred. I did not look back. I didn't need to, because I heard their footsteps following me.

Suddenly, I was the leader. And I understood why: I had walked this route the day before and I knew the way.

We all took in the view. The bridge, in short stretches, spanned high above the ground. Once, I looked back and saw Caleb leaning over the side, peering down at what appeared more like deep wells than anything else. The walls closing in these deep ditches did not allow much light to reach the bottom, so it was sometimes difficult to discern it.

Caleb leaned against the railing and peered off into the distance. "There's the cave."

"Yes; it appears smaller than it actually is," I said. "We are still a half mile away."

"I know," acknowledged Caleb. "Believe me, I know."

We walked the half-mile, rose up through the cave along the spiraling ramp, and found ourselves at the end, standing in the soft sand or ash, in total darkness. I knew a torch burned up ahead, because I saw its faint glow, which served as a beacon.

"Follow me," I said. "Grab on to my shirt and follow me."

We took small steps in the death-like darkness, our shoes making a soft abrading sound in the loose material on the ground.

I walked with my arms out at full length in front of me and my eyes opened as widely as possible to allow whatever light there was into my retinas. As we walked, I could hear Woodgate's breathing, which had the characteristics of congested lungs, possibly asthma.

Eventually, I felt the cool stone against my hands and announced, "Stop."

I turned right, walked more than twenty paces past the torch, and soon began to perceive the hazy light that I knew emanated from the portico stairway. In moments, I felt the cool breezes coming out of the portico.

"Do you feel that?" remarked Woodgate. "A breeze!"

"It feels great on my skin," said Caleb. "Look at that!" As Caleb said this, I felt him release my shirt and then push past me. He ran to the top of the steps, turned around, and announced, "We made it! Come take a look! It's beautiful."

Woodgate released my shirt and walked gingerly toward the light. I decided to stay back and watch. I think that I wanted to view my companions' reactions; appreciate their awe and amazement at the sight of the portico.

Woodgate stood in the diffused light with one hand on his hip and the other in his hair. He was a colorless shadow from my perspective bathed in white light. His head tilted downward as he looked at the marble portico below.

Caleb descended several steps. "What are we waiting for?"

Woodgate followed Caleb, and I followed Woodgate. As our shoes landed silently on the shiny steps, I began to wonder if we were nearing the true end of our journey together. I wondered if I would have the courage to enter that portal. How would Caleb and Woodgate react when they saw the fountain and the tapestries? Would we hear the high-pitched laughter? If so, would that effect a change in my companions? Would they still resolve to open the door to eternity?

I would be lying if I said that my heart was not pounding as I descended those majestic ivory stairs. Woodgate's sudden attempt at levity did not help relieve my anxiety, either.

"Like lambs to slaughter, good men," he said. "Ha-ha—lambs to slaughter."

Chapter Thirty
ETERNITY

THE PORTICO APPEARED EXACTLY as it had the day before. Sunlight illuminated the white surfaces like sunlight on snow. We stood in the middle of the beautiful room, waiting for our eyes to adjust to the light, and taking in the amazing spectacle.

"I almost forgot what civilization was like," said Caleb, in a soft voice.

"This is a colossal find," said Woodgate. "I feel as though I am a few steps from heaven or standing in the chamber of a great Roman Emperor."

I pointed toward the archway that I knew led to the great hall, the fountain, the tapestry, and the portal. "There is more in there."

Caleb and Woodgate shared a look of apprehension, and then began walking alongside me.

Though not dark, the area beneath the archway was shadowed. Emerging from these shadows into the great hall's brilliant light, felt like a rebirth. The fountain immediately caught our attention, its jet shooting 15 feet into the air.

"A cloven jet that does foam and fret," said Woodgate, reciting, rather stiffly, his favorite poem.

I think because I had Woodgate and Caleb with me, I relaxed and soaked in the surroundings more than I had on the day before. I realized, as I surveyed the characteristics of the room, that there was much I had not seen or perceived.

The room was not rectangular, as I had previously believed. It had five sides—an irregular pentagon. The side behind us was the meeting point of two walls. The archway served as the walls' vertex, which I gathered was approximately a 175-degree angle—nearly a straight line. There was nothing ornamental on these two walls, just shiny, white marble. The wall to our left held the tapestries. The wall to the right was made of glass. Water streaked continuously on the other side of this glass. Beyond the water was a light source, choked off at intervals by unseen opaque objects. I surmised that it was sunlight seeping through narrow openings between craggy rocks and then through water, and finally through the smoky glass. This light source created dancing shadows on all surfaces in the room. Of course, when I looked skyward and saw the sun sitting directly above, I decided that the light source behind the glass was more likely manmade or spirit-made.

The fountain gurgled at the center. A purple star-like figure decorated the marble bottom of the fountain's basin. Beneath the constantly moving and bubbling water, this star appeared to dance— to vibrate.

Next to the fountain, on the thirty-foot high wall, were the reddish tapestries. Caleb now stood, gazing fixedly, at the twenty-foot tapestries.

"Amazing," he said, when I walked up beside him. "This one has the withered flowers. Just like the poem said."

"What does it all mean?" said Woodgate, who sidled up beside us.

"It means we have to enter that door," said Caleb. "The door to Mary's garden."

"And what if it does not lead to Mary's garden?" I asked.

Caleb exhaled through pursed lips and shook his head in amusement. He put a hand on each of our shoulders. "Then we are dead," he said. "And the way I see it, we're dead anyway."

"You're talking nonsense," said Woodgate gruffly.

The wall that held the door that my comrades referred to as the "Portal to Eternity" had a shimmering surface that I suddenly realized was actually a great mirror. Caleb, Woodgate, and I stood in front of this great mirror, mesmerized by our appearances. This was Caleb's eighth week on the island, and his change in appearance startled him.

"My hair is all scruffy, my uniform dirty and rumpled," Caleb said as he pushed back his hair and then tried to straighten the wrinkles on his shirt.

"You look fine, Caleb," I said.

"Be thankful neither of you has a whisker on your face," said Woodgate, who was rubbing his hand over the thick black stubble he had grown.

Caleb took off his spectacles and cleaned them with his shirttail.

"I may not have a beard," he acknowledged, "but I can tell I've aged—I've changed in these two months."

"I have changed too, but more on the inside," I said. Caleb smiled, gently patted me on the back, and then put on his spectacles.

"How can you change, Caleb?" said Woodgate. "Dead people can't change, can they?"

Caleb's silence encouraged Woodgate to continue.

"Weren't you the one laughing like a lunatic only an hour ago and singing a song about our status as specters?" Woodgate cleared his throat. "Tell me, what is going to happen when we walk through that door? Are we going to disappear? Evaporate like a puddle in a desert? Perhaps we'll simply grow wings and fly heavenward."

Caleb looked at Woodgate with an amused expression. Though Woodgate was new—in relative time—to us, we both understood his personality and his tendencies. He was a blow-hard—a pirate on the outside, a mermaid on the inside. Caleb began laughing.

"What?" Woodgate's feelings were rankled.

"You—that's what!" Caleb laughed anew, slapping his thigh and shaking his head. I laughed too, but out of respect did my very best to disguise my laughter by putting my hand over my mouth.

Singing.

High, soft, and sweet. A voice seemed to emanate from above—muffled and in a language that I could not discern. We all stood still, as if standing on thin ice. Any wrong move, I felt, might send us crashing.

A bell.

Far off in the distance. It clanged repeatedly, growing quieter and quieter with each passing clang.

"A ship's bell," I said in a whisper.

The soprano voice continued to trill and glide up and down the musical scale. The voice's ethereal energy fell on us like soft light from stars.

"What do we do?" Caleb asked Woodgate.

"Remarkable," said Woodgate, looking up through the open space above us. The sky was a brilliant blue, and puffy white clouds chugged by slowly.

"What do we do?" asked Caleb more urgently.

Woodgate looked down, smiled, and then brought his right hand up to scratch the side of his head. "I suppose we do what we came here to do, Caleb. We walk through the door—the portal—and enter eternity."

The ominous door stood in the dark shadows of an archway, a doorknob at its center. The doorknob, constructed of highly polished gold, was five inches in diameter.

I watched Caleb, dressed in those peculiar green clothes and wearing those bulky black boots, bravely stride into the shadows beneath the archway and put his hand on the doorknob. Woodgate and I remained several paces behind him. Caleb, with his hand wrapped around the golden knob, turned his head and raised his eyebrows. "Are you guys ready?"

We each nodded our heads.

Caleb turned the knob and then I heard the mechanisms inside disengage—it sounded like a gunshot. Then he pushed on the door, and it glided quietly outward, as if the ponderous door were weightless. As it opened, great rays of warm, bright sunlight streamed into the room. Wide enough for all three of us to stand shoulder-to-shoulder-to-shoulder beneath its jamb, the door silently disappeared from view as it turned out to the right.

Chapter Thirty-One
CLANGS AND COLORS

HOW FUNNY WE MUST HAVE LOOKED the moment the cave door swung open—three souls, each dressed in the garb of his own distinct time period, all slack-mouthed, squinting amid the sunbeams, desperately scouring the landscape for signs of Mary in her pleasant garden, or for golden stairs that ascended into the heavens, or for a simple signpost that read, "This way to eternity—mind your step."

The view was stunning, majestic, extraordinary—though there was nothing supernatural about it, at least not that I could immediately discern.

The blue horizon met with the wide expanse of a calm turquoise sea. The rocky slope of the volcanic mountain funneled down to this sea, along which I spied a quaint seaside village.

Civilization!

Large ships, their sails billowing in the breeze, sat docked along a wooden wharf where village met sea. A raised timber walkway radiated out from the wharf, forming a labyrinth of narrow alleys abutted by small village houses—hovels, really. Black iron pipes emitting blue-white smoke jutted at odd angles from the gray rooftops of these crooked houses. A medley of dotted colors moved along the twisted thoroughfare and connected alleyways of the seaside village.

People!

Hundreds of people in variegated clothing milled about like a confused army of parrots. Disappointingly, I could not discern any details beyond the fact that these dots of moving colors were indeed people. I wanted to know at once their nationality, their era, and their language. And then, feeling insignificant, I imagined that the three of us, standing with mouths agape under the lintel of the cave door, must appear to the villagers below as ants do clinging to a shadowy valley in the bark of a great pine tree.

We could walk to this village by first stepping down from the marble stoop in front of the yawning cave door. There our feet would meet the top-most stair of a set of granite steps, piled higgledy-piggledy on each other. The granite stairway ended about halfway to sea level, and thereafter began a snaking gentle path that years of footfalls had worn into the sandy, nearly shrub-free, landscape. This path ended at a small set of timber stairs that rose to the village boardwalk.

Gazing over my shoulder, I estimated that the peak of the volcano loomed 500 feet above us—I was closer than I preferred to be to its boiling spout.

I heard the mewling of many seagulls in the distance, and looking down toward the village, saw their white feather-slim bodies diving and rising in the salty air. I watched as a wooden ship, not unlike the *Bonhomme Richard*, clanged its bell as its sails tightened in the wind, and then, listing from side-to-side, it separated from the village wharf, the prow pointed toward the deep blue hues of the open water beyond the harbor.

The village, I realized, was flanked on each side by two enormous hills—sheer and rocky—that connected to the colossal volcanic mountain, thereby shutting off the village from the rest of the island. I concluded that there were but two ways to enter the village below: by sea via a ship or the way we just had traveled, on foot through the mountain and down the steep hillside.

"So much for Mary's garden," said Woodgate, his voice dry and weak.

"No kidding," agreed Caleb.

"Foolish to believe that Yeats had anything to do with this island," said Woodgate, dejectedly.

Another ship, a slender frigate, hoisted its sails and then eased away from the wharf as a great mob gathered to give, presumably, the ship a celebratory sendoff. I remember thinking that that handsome vessel glided on the serene water like a brittle brown leaf being blown across winter ice.

Caleb asked, "What now? Do we continue? Go back? What?"

None of us spoke, though I did hear Woodgate grunt softly as a way of acknowledging Caleb's questions.

Caleb placed his big heavy hand on my shoulder. "What do you say, boss? What's our next move?"

The frigate's bell clanged loudly, as the handsome broad-sailed craft grew smaller and smaller in its approach of the horizon. Back on the wharf, the colorful gathering of people decreased as the thoroughfare and alleyways filled with the strolling citizens.

I pointed in the direction of the village. "I say we explore . . . and . . . perhaps get some answers."

"You might not like the answers," said Woodgate, heavily.

"It matters not," I said, stepping down onto the granite stairway, "because I do not like the questions anymore."

Chapter Thirty-Two
MISTY VILLAGE HARBOR

YOU NEVER ACTUALLY SEE GRASS GROWING, yet over time it will rise above your knees. It's difficult to perceive the spinning of the Earth as it marks time in gradations of light and dark, yet Mother Earth continues to rotate. A person changes incrementally too. But, when change is happening to you, oftentimes others recognize it before you do. It was this way with me. Standing atop of the marble stoop, looking down at the village, Caleb conferred on me the responsibility of deciding our next move, a decision I made with self-confidence and no self-consciousness. As I alighted from the marble stoop and began a steadfast descent, I realized, too, that I had just dismissed Woodgate's ominous statement, about "not liking the answers," with a pithy declaration of my own that did not include the honorific title "sir."

Seemingly, in the time it took for the ponderous cave door to swing open, I grew from a boy to a man. An equal. Of course, now many years later, I can reflect on this ostensibly miraculous transition and realize that Woodgate and Caleb's feelings toward me did not change so much as my own feelings about myself changed. There was something about making it through the volcanic cave, something about stepping out onto that stoop, something about facing my greatest fears that engendered in me a deeper understanding of myself, of my innate courage, that allowed me to hold my chin up a little higher, expand my chest, and speak a little louder. I would never be as boastful as the chanticleer, for it is not in my nature, but, looking back on that moment, I realize that there was a strut to the way I walked.

The uneven stairs required great concentration, and so after Caleb passed me, I remained head-down, feeling my way, maintaining my balance on the loose steps, completely unaware of Caleb's progress in front of me.

When I stepped onto the gravel and grass path, where the granite stairs ended, Caleb was nowhere in sight.

"Prescott. Over here!" Gazing left, I saw Caleb, some fifty or more feet from the path, sitting upon a granite bench in the shade of a rocky overhang, beckoning me with a wave of his hand.

When I reached him, he handed me his canteen. I sat down on the bench next to Caleb, and drank deeply.

Now more than halfway to sea level, I could make out signs on taverns and other buildings, and a great wooden sign at the wharf with the words "Misty Village" carved into it.

"A ship just pulled into port," said Caleb.

"I saw that."

"It's strange, though." Caleb turned toward me. "Prescott, you're a sailing man. You've been on a ship like that one." I nodded to show my agreement. "Tell me this: how many crewmen does it take to sail a ship like that?"

"I don't know? Ten or fifteen, I would say, at the very least. There is so much to do . . ."

"OK, well, I've been watching that ship, and not one person has come off of it. It appears to be empty."

"That is impossible!" I peered down at the ship, which was now in the shadow of an immense fair-weather cloud.

"I figured at first that there must be a quarantine or something, but that would mean the passengers and crew would have to stay on board—but there's no one."

"There must be someone." I continued studying the ship.

"Yeah," said Caleb, "but there isn't."

"Lads!" It was Woodgate's voice, and it sounded far away. Caleb and I turned toward the path and there was Woodgate, about two hundred yards below us. He had walked right past us. "What are you doing? Trying to lose me?"

Caleb and I immediately began laughing.

"We've been trying to lose you ever since you arrived, Woody," said Caleb loud enough for only me to hear. "But you're like a bad penny."

Woodgate stood with his hands at his sides, his head tilted to the left. Too far away to read the manner of his facial features, I nevertheless pictured his ferret-like face wearing a frown.

"Come on up," said Caleb, now standing and waving. "Get out of the sun." Then Caleb spoke under his breath, "You goofball Englishman."

Woodgate shook his head with disgust and then began marching up the grass and gravel path. At the foot of the stairs, just as he turned right and began walking toward us, he barked, "Were you two going to let me waltz into town alone?"

Caleb and I looked at each other and then burst out laughing. I don't know whether we laughed because we felt guilty for forgetting about Woodgate or whether the notion of Woodgate walking into Misty Village alone rang as funny in our heads. It was likely a little bit of both.

"Laugh all you want, lads," Woodgate said, now smiling. "I'm on to you. You want me to be the guinea pig, eh? Let old Woody walk into town, and see if he gets strung up, or lit on fire, or cannibalized. Brilliant. Simply brilliant."

Picturing these horrible scenarios, for some odd reason, was hilarious to us, and we laughed uproariously.

Woodgate chuckled. "You love a lark, don't you, Caleb, especially if it involves me being tortured." Woodgate then gestured for me to hand him the canteen, which I did, laughing all the while. Woodgate drank deeply, and then looked down at the seaside village.

All laughter had subsided, and then it was quiet enough to hear the light sea breeze riffling as it passed through the nearby foliage. "So, what do you make of it—the village, the ships, the people? What will happen when we come waltzing into town?"

"Time will tell," said Caleb.

"I have a crazy theory I'd like to share with you," said Woodgate, handing back the canteen to me, which I then passed to Caleb.

"A theory, huh?" said Caleb. "About what?"

"That village. This island," said Woodgate. "I don't think it's a very good theory, but . . ."

"OK, I'll ask: what's your theory?" Caleb looked up at Woodgate, who held his arms akimbo and twisted his torso, seemingly to stretch the muscles in his back.

Woodgate squatted down and rested on his calves. "Well, what if this island . . . what if we aren't supposed to be here . . . what if we came here by mistake? And what if we we're supposed to walk through the volcanic mountain and come to this village? And, what if we're supposed to get on one those ships and go home?"

"And what if monkeys are supposed to fly out of my butt?" said Caleb.

No one laughed.

"It's a theory—just pitching it out there."

"All right," said Caleb, standing up. "I'll play along. Let's imagine we waltz into town, as you put it, and find out it's 1916. How does Prescott get back to 1779? And, what about me? Do I wait around for 50 years before boarding a ship?"

"What about the French woman?" Woodgate said to Caleb. "She's from a time after you. She dreamed of a ship that would take her home. She was drawn inland, probably to this village."

"She could be down there," I said, excitedly.

"Yes," said Woodgate. "Or she could have sailed away on one of those ships. Don't you see? All evidence indicates to us that people have been coming to this island in droves, walking down that path, coming through that door in the mountain. They can't all be down there. This would be a colossal city, not a small seaside village. No, they have to be sailing away. The question is: where do they go?"

"It's a beautiful little town," I said.

"Yes," said Woodgate. "It is . . ."

"Gorgeous!" said Caleb, but there was something strange in his voice, a lifting inflection that didn't sound like he was finishing Woodgate's statement. Then I realized that Caleb was not looking at the village; he faced the grass and gravel path, instead.

Men have a way of becoming dumb whenever in the presence of a beautiful woman. When ambushed by beauty, something catches the tongue, ties it in a knot, and turns the brain to cornmeal. Caleb saw her first. I saw her next, and when I did, I nudged Woodgate, whose slack jaw and pie plate eyes informed me of his astonishment in seeing her too.

Seagulls mewled noisily above.

Radiant light reflected off of her white dress.

Chapter Thirty-Three
FOLLOWING

"OH!" UTTERED THE YOUNG GIRL in the shimmering white dress; obviously startled at seeing us, she quickly raised her hand to cover her mouth and threw the other hand out to help maintain balance, as if she were standing on thin ice. "You frightened me." Her shoulders relaxed and she leaned over and released a ripple of embarrassed laughter.

What a beautiful smile. What a kind smile.

The girl's dress was only long enough to cover her thighs, and there were no sleeves—her arms were bare! This risqué ensemble embarrassed me, and it was difficult for me, at first, to look at anything but her face, which was beautiful. Her chestnut brown hair was pulled back in a neat bun, and though she stood twenty feet from me, I noticed and admired her large blue eyes, full red lips, and milky-white skin. Around her neck, she wore a colorful silk scarf, with orange, purple, and black designs.

Caleb stood up straight and began pressing his hands against his wrinkled uniform.

Something suddenly changed in her eyes. The fear disappeared, the muscles in her face relaxed, and she managed a coy smile—brilliant white teeth indicated to me that this young lady was also likely from Caleb's time period.

"You guys frightened me," she said again in a gentle voice. Her voice evoked a reaction in me that is difficult to explain. I felt an aberrant longing, perhaps because I had not heard a woman's voice in a long, long time.

"I'm sorry," said Caleb. "We didn't mean to scare you."

I rose and approached the young lady. I noticed, as I neared her, that she wore very unusual shoes. They were white, ankle-high, and laced over the arch of the foot.

"Prescott Fielding, ma'm," I said, offering her my hand, bowing, and revealing my right calf in the process. She smiled quizzically as she accepted my hand.

Caleb and Woodgate then stepped forward and introduced themselves, and each introduction caused the smiling girl to nod her had and giggle nervously.

"You remind me of a girl I once knew," Woodgate said, her hand in his.

The young lady blushed and giggled timidly.

"May I ask your name?" said Woodgate, still grasping her hand.

"Oh, I'm sorry. Yes. Melanie," she said. "My name is Melanie Simpson."

Her anxious laughter was contagious; we all now laughed at some unknown bit of wit, as if there was something funny in all we said, every action.

"Are you guys on your way to Misty Village?" she asked while withdrawing her hand from Woodgate's sweaty grip. Her accent, I realized, was similar to but not exactly like Caleb's, just as my own accent was similar to but different from Woodgate's.

"Misty Village?" said Woodgate, who obviously had not before noticed the great wooden sign.

"Yes—yes we are—why, are you from there?" said Caleb, eager to converse with this lovely girl.

"Yes and no," she said.

Caleb nodded his head, and I could tell he was too embarrassed to ask for clarification, so I did.

"I am spending some time in Misty Village," she said to us, "but I expect to sail home within the next couple of days."

Woodgate turned to Caleb and me and gave a meaningful look. "Sail home, eh?" he said. "Where is home?"

"California."

"Really?" Woodgate's expression darkened. "This may be perceived as a strange question, and I hope you do not mind me asking it, Melanie. When were you born—what year?"

"Oh." She smiled coyly. "I don't mind. I was born in 1982."

Caleb, Woodgate, and I exchanged acknowledging glances.

"Is everyone in Misty Village sailing to California?" Caleb asked.

Melanie shook her head and giggled. "No! Of course not!"

"Are they all from your time—1982?" I asked.

"No, of course not," Melanie said. "Why would they be?" Something changed in Melanie's face. Was she looking at us with suspicion?

I shrugged my shoulders, and wondered if there was something that I did not understand, but when I glanced at my comrades their concerned faces told me that I was not alone in my confusion.

"Did you come from within the volcano?" Melanie asked.

"Yes," Caleb said. "Did you?"

"No," she said, brusquely, and then exhaling, said, "I'm sorry. Yes, I was up near the volcano, but I did not come from within it."

"What were you doing up there, then?" asked Woodgate.

"I was working . . . look, have you been given any instructions about what to do next?"

"Should we have?" Woodgate asked.

"You're the first person we've seen," explained Caleb.

"We just got here," said Woodgate.

Melanie's eyes followed the granite steps up to the cave door, which was indistinguishable in the mountain's craggy surface, then looked down at Misty Village. Her eyebrows were knitted in concern, and her initial friendliness had changed to the icy demeanor of an overworked Boston merchant.

"I think you guys had better follow me," Melanie said, and then she began briskly walking down the winding gravel and grass path. We immediately fell in behind her, trying to keep pace with her quick strides.

"Where are we going?" demanded Woodgate.

"You'll soon see," she said, all the while walking hurriedly.

"I don't want to see; I would like to know my destination long before arrival!" Woodgate's demand died on the salt air. Melanie continued walking without a response.

When, some ten minutes later, the grass and gravel path met a raised wooden boardwalk, Melanie jumped up, two steps at a time, while Woodgate intermittently implored, "Miss? Are you going to answer me? Are you ignoring me, Miss? Miss?"

It was comical watching Woodgate desperately try to catch up with Melanie, waving his arms in the air to emphasize his words.

Caleb and I walked side-by-side. I asked, "What do you think?"

"I don't know what to think anymore," he said. "Look at this place!"

Gray wooden houses filled all possible space to the left and the right of the boardwalk. People, wearing clothing from across the centuries, walked among us. Each house was uniform in size and structural design—a gray door at the center, a four-paned glass window to each side of the door, and one four-paned glass window near the peak of the roof. Each house produced a different cooking scent: we passed fish frying, stews boiling, pastry baking, and pork broiling. The faces in the crowd were friendly and of different ages and ethnicities. People nodded to us as we passed, but did not speak to us.

Melanie's long strides carried her deep into the thickening crowd. I feared we would lose sight of her if she quickened her pace anymore. Then, as I contemplated this notion, I also thought of suggesting to Caleb and Woodgate that we discontinue following her, but that was when a haggard old woman, in a gray dress, tailored to her fat ankles, arrested Melanie's progress. I looked up, past the white corrugated apron over the old woman's gray dress, past her thick waist, above her large, misshapen bosom, and settled on her wrinkled, hatchet face. Melanie spoke to this woman and then pointed in our direction. The old woman followed Melanie's outstretched arm and her hawk eyes landed on Caleb.

"We've been spotted, gentlemen," Caleb said, half jokingly.

The old woman raised her hand and waved to us; beckoned us to come closer.

Suddenly, Melanie was no longer our guide. As a matter of fact, Melanie was gone. I assumed she had disappeared in the increasingly thickening crowd.

"Follow me," said the old woman. She walked at an easier pace, and soon I was standing directly behind her.

"May I ask you where you are leading us, ma'am?" I said in a voice that was enveloped by the din produced by the noisy villagers, each conversing about comings and goings, ships and voyages, food and drink, and reuniting with friends, relatives and loved ones. I caught snatches of conversation as they all walked past me. Where they were going was a mystery to me. We had just traveled the boardwalk, bordered by house after house and no walkways jutting off to either side, so I knew the residents' options were limited to walking to a house and entering it, or walking to the sandy path that leads up to the granite steps and, eventually, the volcanic cave.

The old woman chose not to answer my question in words; instead, she simply pointed to a large, white building with a spire roof.

We reached an open area where hundreds of villagers milled about. From here, wooden boardwalks radiated off in many directions. The tall ships were to our left, bobbing and rocking in the harbor tide. I nudged Caleb, and nodded my head toward the grand ship. I wanted him to see that sailors now carried massive trunks on their shoulders and walked up long, steep wooden ramps that rose to the main deck of the ships. I noticed that the black trunks each had "*U.S.S. Triumph*" inscribed on them in gold letters.

"It's not a ghost ship after all," I said.

Caleb squinted and shook his head suspiciously. "I don't know, Pres."

The old woman abruptly stopped, and I nearly bumped into her large backside. She raised her hand again and pointed to our right.

"The grim reaper tells us to go to that building," said Caleb, in a voice that most assuredly reached the old woman's ears; however, she gave no indication that the comments affected her.

Caleb and Woodgate began striding toward the large, white building, which Caleb said looked like his "town hall." I remained behind and made one last attempt to converse with this woman.

"Prescott Fielding, my lady," I said, offering her my hand, bowing, and displaying my calf. "And how may I call you?"

She huffed and puffed, and then reluctantly accepted my hand. Her clammy and pudgy hand felt like a piece of underdone pork.

"Betsy McDuffy," she said in a surprisingly gentle voice, and then she released my hand. "Now be on your way, boy."

Betsy McDuffy walked away, eventually blending in with the village crowd.

"What a lovely, charming, gentle lady," I said to myself, dripping with sarcasm. I then jogged to catch up with my mates.

The afternoon sun waned and a stiff breeze blew out to sea. I passed a cluster of young men, dressed in black suits and carrying black canes. The men spoke of "times of embarkation" and hopes of "smooth sailing." I assumed these men would board the ship that sat docked several hundred feet behind me. I also assumed that it was their trunks that the sailors carried aboard, and that they would set sail this evening.

I met up with Woodgate and Caleb in front of a well manicured lawn surrounded by a neat, white picket fence.

"It's strange," said Woodgate, "the way we've been treated—like cattle being mindlessly moved from one point to another."

Caleb and I agreed with Woodgate.

"I don't like it," said Caleb.

A narrow brick walkway led to the white building. Constructed on a small hill, the building was trimmed in forest green paint: green shutters, green awnings, a green door, and a six-inch green trim that ran below the roof.

"What do we do now?" I asked.

"Knock on the door. See what happens," Caleb said.

Woodgate unlatched the gate, pushed it aside, and walked up the brick walkway.

"I'll take a good hot meal, a bath, and a soft place to sleep over information, at this point," said Woodgate, as he reached out and pressed a button on the house, which produced a bell-like sound inside the house.

In a moment, we heard footsteps from within, and the slow unlatching of many locks on the door.

Chapter Thirty-Four
THE CLERK OF THE WORKS

IT TOOK NEARLY A MINUTE—a minute!—for the person behind the door to disengage what seemed like a dozen locks and fasteners. When the door began to pull back into the building, I felt Woodgate and Caleb bear in more closely on me; we all leaned forward out of curiosity. I could make out a wall not very far behind the door—it was not a large room—and some wooden shelves with large tin cups stacked on them. Then I looked down and saw a little old man about five feet tall, stooped over with age, bald-headed, with two loop earrings in one ear, and wearing spectacles on the end of his long nose.

"Oh!" he said, as he looked up at us. "Welcome! Welcome! Come on in!"

I stepped aside and let Woodgate enter first, not because I was being gallant and not because I was afraid to enter. I did this so that I could make eye contact with Woodgate. I wanted to gauge his reaction, which, with raised eyebrows and a slightly upturned mouth, mirrored my own reaction.

The room was unspectacular; a box surrounded by dusty shelves behind a storefront counter that was also covered with dust. To the right behind the counter were shelves built onto a door. I discerned the doorknob between the third and fourth shelf from the ceiling. On one of the shelves, between brass bookends shaped liked lions, I saw several volumes of books, bound in leather. The titles I could not make out, but I saw a familiar name on each spine—Yeats.

"Follow me, gentlemen," the little man said. He walked behind the counter, placed his mottled-brown hand between two shelves, and twisted the doorknob. The door swung into the room, revealing a dark, narrow hallway. The little man walked into the darkness. I heard him grope around, rubbing his hand against the wall, and then he flipped a switch, and a long line of tubes in the ceiling illuminated the hallway.

There was nothing remarkable about this hallway, except that it was much longer than I would have thought possible, judging by what I perceived of the size of the house from outside. Wide pine boards, dark and splintered, ran parallel to the corridor. The white plastered walls, decorated with cobwebs, scuff marks, and holes, met a tiled, yellow ceiling.

The little old man's gait was comical. He carried his hands in a fist by his hips, stooped over at a 45-degree angle, and carried most of his weight on his left foot, which made him list slightly to the left. I looked at Caleb and smiled. He lifted his palms and shrugged his shoulders, and his face indicated to me that he considered the situation and the little man to be ludicrous and odd. I walked directly behind the man, followed by Woodgate and Caleb. At one point, Woodgate leaned forward and whispered, "Where do you think he's taking us?"

"I am sure it cannot be much farther," I whispered back.

"How do you know?" Woodgate whispered.

I shrugged my shoulders.

The hallway ended at a dilapidated, wooden staircase that rose twenty feet and then disappeared into darkness.

"Oh, terrific!" said Woodgate, no longer whispering. "What I really want to do is more climbing."

The little old man flipped a switch and the stairway became bathed in unnatural light. I looked up and saw that the stairs ended at a wooden ceiling.

"Follow me," said the little old man.

"What—up there?" Woodgate said. "It goes nowhere."

Caleb and I ascended the stairs while Woodgate waited below. "I'll climb when I see there is a way out; otherwise, I'll be down here." Woodgate then muttered several colorful words under his breath.

The little old man reached the ceiling and then pointed upward. "Do me a favor, Mr. Thompson, and help an old man out by pushing up the door."

Caleb stood next to the little old man and pressed his shoulder and hands into the ceiling, which rose and opened outward. We all continued up the stairs and stepped into a great gothic church.

"We're almost there," said the little old man. "You better tell Julian Woodgate to hurry if he wants to be the first in line at the buffet table."

"Wait a minute!" said Caleb in a raised voice.

The little old man froze and then looked up at Caleb.

"How do you know my name?"

"Didn't you tell me your name just a few moments ago?" said the little man.

"I . . ."

"Yes," said the little man, turning and now walking away, "I'm quite sure you did." He continued walking down the center aisle of the magnificent church.

Caleb and I exchanged looks of bewilderment. Then I leaned over the hole in the floor to call to Woodgate, but when I did, he was already two-thirds of the way up. Red-faced and sweating, his handkerchief in his hand, Woodgate did not look happy. But the grimace on his face changed to a look of curiosity and amazement when he soaked in the surroundings.

The church—the dark wooden pews, the high decorative columns, the red carpeting, and the stained glass windows—Woodgate later told me that reminded him of the Anglican church he attended in Oxford.

The little old man, limping slowly down the center aisle, stepped up onto the altar and then turned around.

"You want to eat? Hurry up!" he said in a squeaky voice that echoed throughout the building.

Woodgate looked confused. His attention had been entirely consumed by the visual splendor inside the church—he stood there rotating while gazing up at the vaulted ceilings.

"He's going to feed us," said Caleb to Woodgate.

"Something about a buffet," I explained.

"Well then," said Woodgate, releasing the top button on his shirt, "What are we waiting for?"

"Something else," said Caleb, arresting Woodgate's progress by grasping him by the wrist. "He knows our names."

"What?"

"He called me Mr. Thompson and you Julian Woodgate," explained Caleb.

"What about Prescott?" Woodgate nodded toward me.

"I do not know?" I said.

"Really, gentlemen," came the echoing old voice from the altar. "We must move along."

The little old man pushed an ornate door, gilded with angels and other religious icons, into a pocket in the wall. As we approached, he stepped to the side and made an awkward bow. "After you, gentlemen, and, er, the fine young boy."

We were outside. Three granite steps led to a mosaic floor of blue and white marble. Torches burned around the perimeter, as it was now rather dark. Great flames rose from metallic boxes in front of us, and men, wearing puffy white hats, worked with great speed and agility above the flames, turning great pieces of beef and pork on grated metal. A gathering of very well dressed men and women sat at an oval table. Tall glasses of red wine in their hands, they laughed and chatted and toasted one another in exaggerated and animated gestures. The men wore black suits and white shirts—tuxedos, Caleb called them—and the women wore beautiful white-laced dresses. A small group of musicians—a drummer who sat while he played, a violinist, several guitarists, and a man playing a rather large harpsichord that I later learned was a pianoforte—performed a kind of music I had never before heard, but it was pleasing to the ear nevertheless. After one song ended and a new one began, several men rose from their seats and each took the hand of a woman, and then led her out to the open area between us and their table. Then they proceeded to dance in a most elegant manner; each woman held a man's outstretched hand and each wrapped the other hand around the back of their partner.

The little old man pushed between us, as we stood with our mouths agape at this scene, and stepped down the three steps onto the marble floor.

"Your table is over here, gentlemen," he said, and pointed to a small round table just a few feet from the band.

We sat, ate a delicious array of food: salad, carrots, asparagus, potatoes, beef, pork, bread, soup, pudding, and several pots of piping hot tea. After the main course, a tall man with a stiff gait and an upturned nose promenaded over and placed a bottle of red wine on our table. But only Woodgate indulged.

Later, the musicians swiftly packed their instruments and equipment and disappeared into the darkness. With no music, the revelers in the tuxedos and gowns also scattered like dandelion spores in a gentle breeze. Soon, all was quiet. That was when the little man returned and took a seat across from me at the table.

"Tomorrow morning, gentlemen, you will return home," he announced confidently. His face was half in shadow as the other half flickered in the torchlight.

"What?" I said.

"Return home? Are you joking?" said Caleb.

"I'm not joking, Caleb. You are going home," he said gently.

"How do you know my name? And who are you to tell me where I'm going?"

"Did you enjoy your meal?" the little man said, giving no indication that Caleb's tone of voice intimidated him.

"Answer me!" said Caleb, sitting up suddenly.

"Relax, Caleb. Relax!" the old man said.

"Relax?" Caleb reached over and squeezed the man's pullover with his forefinger and thumb. "What do you say you level with us, huh?"

The old man blinked and swallowed hard. "All right," he said. "Unhand me and I will tell you everything you want to know."

Caleb released his grip. He was breathing hard and greatly agitated. The man brushed down the wrinkle in his pullover with his hand. "It's not as if I am keeping anything from you," muttered the little old man.

"Well?" said Caleb.

"I know who you are, Caleb, because it is my job to do so," he said.

"And what job is that?" said Woodgate.

"I'm the Misty Village clerk," he said with a smile. "I'm the clerk of the works, you could say."

"A clerk?" I said. "So how is it you know our names?"

"Well, it's my job to know," he said, looking at me with squinted eyes, as though something about my face bothered him.

"We've already covered that ground, old man," said Caleb, his shoulders straightening out.

The old man waved his tiny hand to signal Caleb to calm down and then leaned back into his chair. "I manage this village. The ships come in and out—you know—bringing in supplies and bringing out people." He pulled his glasses off of his face, blew on them, and then put them back on the end of his nose. The odd thing was that he did not appear to even look through the lenses. "It's my job to know what is coming and who is going." He leaned forward. "I get a list!" He emphasized this last remark by lightly snapping his fingers.

What he meant by "a list," escaped all of us.

Chapter Thirty-Five
THREE KEYS

THE THREE OF US SAT AT THE TABLE for nearly an hour that night, sipping tea in the flickering torchlight and throwing questions at the little old man. In that time we learned the little old man's name was Trent Cepulinski. He hailed from St. Paul, Minnesota. He looked more than eighty years old, though he would not tell us specifically what age he had attained, because "a gentleman never reveals all his cards." Trent arrived at the island forty years ago, but he never gave us a clear understanding of what conveyed him here. "I floated here . . . well, and landed over there on the north beach—you know—and followed the path—you know—to Misty Village," he said.

Trent knew much more about the mechanisms and mysteries of the island, but he was reluctant to reveal too much. I asked him what year Misty Village was founded, and his response was, "It's been here since time immemorial." Caleb asked to know the purpose of the island and the village, but Trent skirted the issue like a wily politician. "The purpose of the island is to bring resolve to otherwise unresolved situations."

We learned that the first building we entered was his living quarters. He explained that the storefront had many secret doors in the shelving, and that his living quarters were to the right. We learned that he built the house into the side of a hill. The long, narrow hallway we had traversed actually burrowed deep into that hill and out the other side and then beneath the cathedral.

Woodgate wondered what life he would return to, and Trent winked at Woodgate and said, "Whatever life you want to return to." Trent was very relaxed when he spoke with Caleb and Woodgate; but when I asked questions, something in him tensed up, as if he could not predict what I would say, or he feared that I would ask him something that he could not or did not want to answer.

"There is much here—you know—to enjoy," Trent said, winking at Caleb and Woodgate. "Eat, drink, and be merry."

Trent would not expound about the aforementioned list, except to say that, "It tells me who is coming and when they are going. It is very accurate." He would not reveal who makes the list or where it comes from.

"I have three keys here," Trent said, patting his trouser pocket. "You fellows should return to the village—you know—for a well-deserved respite. You will stay at the Sparrow Inn, on the dock."

Trent could not whisk away Caleb that easily. I could see that Caleb was tense. Woodgate, after the long day's walk and several glasses of red wine, did not seem to be following the conversation. But Caleb was concentrating on every word, analyzing every gesture and inflection. There was no show of excitement in Caleb over the prospect of going home. He needed to know more.

"Have you been in the volcano?" Caleb asked Trent.

"Yes."

"The marble room inside?"

"Yes."

"Did you see the fountain and the tapestries?"

"Yes."

"What can you tell us about it?"

Trent smiled coyly and then reached into his trouser pockets. "There are many mysteries on this island. I am—you know—the clerk of the works, not the Almighty All Knowing." Trent laughed the strangest little laugh—his throat gurgled and spittle drooled down the side of his mouth.

"Look at the stars in the sky," Trent said, jangling several metallic objects in his hand. "Do you know why they are there? Who put them in the sky?" He blinked his eyes slowly, smacked his lips, and then looked over at the exhausted Woodgate. "You should go now—rest."

We stood up and waited for Trent to rise slowly from his seat. He revealed three silver keys in his hand. "One for you, Caleb—room

212. One for you, Woodgate—room 213. And one for you—ah—room 214."

He didn't know my name. The little devil didn't know my name. He had been looking at me sideways all night, possibly wracking his tiny brain for an answer that would not arrive. I bothered him. Not knowing my name rattled him. Perhaps, I was not supposed to be here. His special "list" could not account for me.

This oversight might have angered me, but I decided to use it to my advantage.

"Mr. Cepulinski," I said, calmly. The old man gazed up at me: his nose twitching, and his eyes squinting. Caleb and Woodgate turned to me also. "You have not been entirely honest with us tonight, have you?"

"Honest?" he said, kneading his tiny hands in front of his chest. "Whatever do you mean by that, boy—honest?"

"I think there are some things that you do not know about me, and one thing is that I know more than you think I know about this island." I was bluffing. But I reasoned that if this man did not know me, then there was a chance that what he did not know intimidated him. Trent struck me as a person with an endless desire to be in control.

"What are you talking about, Prescott?" said Caleb.

I put my hand out to hold off his question, never taking my eyes away from Trent.

"Ah, Prescott," said Trent, smiling and suddenly relaxed. "You ask very good questions. Very good—you know—questions, indeed. But I have told you everything you need to know. Have I not been—you know—hospitable to you tonight?"

"Are we dead, Mr. Cepulinski?" I said in as serious voice as I could muster. I trained my eyes on his, watching every twitch in his sallow face. Trent's eyes wavered to the left and right. He looked up at Woodgate and Caleb. This question agitated him. He tugged at his pullover with one hand and opened and closed his fist repeatedly in his other hand.

"Nonsense!" he said. "You gentlemen can leave through that gate. It will bring you out to the street. Follow the street to the dock and the Sparrow Inn." Trent then labored up the three granite steps and leaned against the door to the cathedral's altar.

"He is a coward," I said, as the old man disappeared into the church.

"What's up with you, man?" said Caleb, laughing.

"I have a bad feeling," I said.

"He's an annoying old man, but I think he's harmless," said Caleb. "What about you, Woodgate? What do you think?"

"I think I need to sleep on it," he said, yawning.

We began walking along a cobblestone walkway, lined on both sides at intervals of four or five feet with ankle-high gas lamps and flanked on the right by a towering stonewall. I heard the familiar sounds of the ocean before I saw the moonlight glittering on the water, and then looking to my left, noticed the skeletal outline of the ropes, spars, and masts. The post-and-beam fence in front of us separated the path and a thirty foot drop onto the rocky harbor.

Connected to this post-and-beam fence was a weathered stockade fence, more than six feet in height. Nailed to the fence was a sign that I could easily read in the moonlight: "No Trespassing. Per Order of The Clerk of the Works." A tree with low branches grew next to the fence, which connected to the large stone wall we had just passed, and I was inclined to climb the tree and satisfy my curiosity about what lay beyond the fence; however, I resisted and reluctantly turned left and joined Woodgate and Caleb in our quest to find the Sparrow Inn.

Soon we were at the dock, where a group of more than fifty people stood waving handkerchiefs and hats as the ship that I had seen sailors loading earlier that day silently sailed out to sea. On the deck of the ship stood the men in tuxedos and the women in ball gowns that had danced behind the cathedral an hour ago. One man stood up on the rail at the stern of the ship, a great smile on his face, and took off his hat, pressed it to his chest, and then made a gallant bow. This act evoked a roar of cheers from the crowd.

"I wouldn't want to sail on a foggy night like tonight," said Woodgate, yawning.

"No kidding," said Caleb. "You could end up running into a sand bar and going down like the *Triumph*."

"*Triumph?*" I said, searching my mind for a meaning to that term.

"Yes, old sport," said Woodgate. "The *Triumph* was a late 19th century luxury ship that hit an iceberg on its maiden voyage and sank to the bottom of the sea—hundreds died in the frigid waters."

"Sank?"

"Quite right," said Woodgate, now yawning loudly. "And now, good men, I am going to sleep. Adieu." Then he approached a small group of young ladies conversing beneath a nearby lamppost. "Would you be kind enough to point me in the direction of the Sparrow Inn, my dears?"

Without turning to look at Woodgate, one young lady raised her arm and pointed the way.

"Much obliged," said Woodgate, bowing again and then winking to us as he slowly turned on his heels and walked away. He listed a little as he walked, which I attributed to the effects of the wine he consumed, and he limped slightly.

Caleb slapped me on the chest with the back of his hand, said, "let's go," and then jogged off to catch up with Woodgate.

I turned to the gathering of young ladies standing in the weak lamplight, and became unnerved when I noticed that one girl among the clique fixed her eyes on me—a wide-eyed stare that implied a mixed message. Was it fear I saw in those eyes . . . or malice? Feeling self-conscious, I lowered my eyes and began walking toward the inn, but stole several furtive glances toward that young lady before entering the Sparrow Inn. Each time I looked back, her eyes were upon me. Her face looked familiar, but I did not put a name to the face until later when I was pulling down the blankets on the bed in room 214 of the Sparrow Inn. It was Melanie Simpson, the beautiful young girl who had met us on the hillside and led us into Misty Village to Betsy McDuffy, the haggard old lady on the boardwalk.

Chapter Thirty-Six
TRESSPASSING

I DID NOT SLEEP WELL THAT NIGHT, despite my exhaustion. Bells rang on the hour, as I deduced more ships left the harbor carrying hundreds of passengers eager to see home again.

After several hours of lying in bed staring at the darkened ceiling, I decided that sleep would not arrive for me until I satisfied a particular curiosity that had been nagging at me ever since we departed from the little dinner party with Trent Cepulinski.

I dressed in the dark, pulled on my shoes, placed my room key in my waistcoat pocket, and exited the room. Daylight was breaking, but it was still dark enough to move stealthily past the wooden docks and gangplanks. As I rapidly strode by the ships moored to the docks I saw only one soul, a silhouette of a sailor sitting atop of a trunk, and I would not have noticed him if it were not for the orange glow of his cigarette brightening as he smoked it.

Several hundred feet away from the smoking sailor, the coastline began to rise gently, creating rocky cliffs, which necessitated the post-and-beam fence that connected to the stockade fence, the one with the no trespassing sign nailed to it.

I quickly peered over my shoulder to confirm that I was not being trailed by anyone, and satisfied that I was alone, hurriedly walked into the shadows and grasped onto the tree that grew alongside the stockade fence. It took very little effort to climb ten feet into the tree, and then while holding onto a branch, I placed my foot on the top of the fence. I noticed a small platform on the opposite side of the fence, built, I imagined, for a guard to stand upon so that it was possible to see over the fence. Still holding to the tree for balance, I managed to alight upon this platform, and then, after a few nimble moves, I was on the ground, officially trespassing.

The coastline path descended slightly, and led down to an abandoned dock very similar to the one outside the Sparrow Inn. I rounded a corner alongside the great stonewall that divided this part of the coastline and the great church behind Cepulinski's living quarters, and the jibs and masts of several ships appeared in view, ghost ships rocking and creaking on the sea. These ships, four or five in number, appeared to be in disuse, abandoned. Old planks boarded up portholes. Canvas sails lay in great piles on the decks. Seagulls roosted in thatched nests on the cabins, deck railings, and crow's nests. The gangplanks, still attached to the ships, were rotted, seemingly forsaken one gloomy day many years ago.

"What is this all about?" I wondered. "Why would these ships be left to molder until ruined and useless?"

I moved closer to the first ship and noticed, in the increasing light, that beneath the bowsprit someone had carved a figurehead of a beautiful woman, painted in bluish-white, and possessing angel wings. A bird's nest, made of sedge grasses and dried sea plants, rested upon the figurehead, creating an unintentional Christ-like crown on the carved figure's delicate head.

Sharp guttural sounds repeated in the distance.

Was a large bird making that noise? No, it was the bark of dogs! Gazing up I realized that two large hunting dogs with pointed bat ears were charging uphill toward me—yapping, grunting, and snarling shadows rushing toward me on four legs.

I backed up a few steps, nearly falling over in my haste, and then turned and frantically sprinted toward the stockade fence where I had entered this cheerless wharf. The barking grew in volume as the dogs quickly gained on me. I could hear huffing and puffing, the clacking and banging of digging claws and heavy paws landing on the hard-packed trail. I leaped up and grasped onto the platform, and hearing the agitated hunters growling directly behind me, pulled myself up like a gymnast, swinging my legs up and over the fence with an agility that belied my true abilities and athleticism.

I picked myself up off the ground, quickly brushed off my trousers, and, as the dogs rumbled the fence and their loud barking rang out across the harbor, I quickly returned to my room in the Sparrow Inn, where I did manage an hour's undisturbed sleep sometime soon after. I should clarify these remarks by stating that I was undisturbed by external noises as I slept; however, those internal machinations of sleep bothered me deeply, as dream after dream ended in a most unusual way.

In one dream I returned to my former home in Boston, Massachusetts, and I eagerly opened the door and found Betsy McDuffy, the haggard old woman in Misty Village, sitting at my table, laughing as she plucked the feathers off a plump chicken.

Then I found myself aboard the *Bonhomme Richard*, in another dream. And when I opened my cabin door, there she was again: McDuffy, lying in my cot, smoking a pipe, and laughing in a maniacal way.

Finally, I dreamt that I sat in a field of high grass. Yellow and white flowers rose above the grass; the splayed out petals were pleasant inns for the bees to alight upon. A gentle breeze whispered through the grass and flowers, passing the perfumes of spring across my nose. And, off in the distance, I saw Melanie approach. She held a bouquet of wild flowers in her hands, and wore the white cotton dress that I had seen her in the day before. She was singing in a beautiful soprano voice—the voice I had heard while standing in the great hall. Her image glinted like glass in the sun. It reminded me of Caleb's metal dog tag chain that caught my attention on my very first day on the island. Melanie's image flashed in and out, and though she walked toward me, she never gained any ground. The sun grew brighter and brighter, until I could no longer see anything. I felt hot and disconnected to anything. I floated in a space of white light and I heard a heart beating—the pounding and pounding of a healthy, young heart.

As often happens, dreams melt into real life. And, as that heart continued to beat, I suddenly became aware of another similar pounding. Someone knocked on my door. It took a moment for me to familiarize myself with my surroundings. I did not know where I was at first. Room 214 was quite dark when I entered it the night before. But now I surveyed the room and saw a small writing table, several paintings of seascapes on the walls, and a chest of drawers with a metal pitcher sitting on it.

The knocks persisted, and I called to the visitor, "I'm coming." I slipped on my shoes, brushed back my hair with my hand, and walked toward the door. I pressed my ear against the door and said, "Who goes there?"

"It's me—Caleb. Open up."

Chapter Thirty-Seven
BON VOYAGE AND GOODBYE

I TURNED THE HANDLE AND THREW OPEN THE DOOR. Caleb stood out in the hallway a transformed man. He had replaced his green wrinkled uniform and black boots with brown trousers, a white shirt, a light brown suit jacket, tan shoes, and a festive blue tie. I hardly recognized him. He turned around a couple of times in the hallway and said, "What do you think of the new threads?"

"They look great, but . . . where did you get them?"

"They were in my room," he said. "I found them on my bed along with this note." He reached into his pocket and presented a hand-written note.

Caleb Thompson,

Please accept these new clothes for your voyage home. Your family and friends greatly anticipate your return. Your ship leaves at noon, tomorrow. Be on the docks no later than 11:30. You will board the "Jupiter Sunset."

Sincerely,
Trent Cepulinski
Clerk of the Works

"I'm not going back to Nam, Prescott!" Caleb said with a broad smile. "I'm going home—to my mom and friends and home cooking and my car and television . . ." Caleb stopped suddenly when he realized I did not share his jubilation. "What's up, Prescott? You'll be going home too, right?"

"Look around," I said. "There is no note and no suit."

"Yes, but Trent will see to it that you go home. It's his job."

Caleb walked into my room and sat on the unmade bed. He looked at my pillow and then patted the mattress. "I had the most amazing dreams last night."

"As did I."

"Really? Then you dreamt of home? Saw all your friends?"

"Well, I . . ."

"Because I had what seemed like a three-hour conversation with my mother," said Caleb in an excited voice. "We talked about all the things I've missed. Do you know my cousin, Sandy, married an inventor from Connecticut? At least that's what my mother told me."

"Knock-knock," said Woodgate, standing at the open door. Woodgate wore a dark suit with a vest and golden pocket watch that he withdrew from his coat pocket. "Eleven O'clock, gentlemen." Woodgate had shaved and parted his hair neatly down the middle.

"You look like a million bucks!" said Caleb, springing from his seat on the bed and rushing over to shake Woodgate's hand.

"You look good enough to bury," joked Woodgate. Caleb released Woodgate's hand and they moved closer to me. "Where are your clothes?"

"He didn't get any," explained Caleb. "Did you get a letter?" Caleb handed over his letter to Woodgate, and Woodgate pulled a similar note from his pocket and handed it to Caleb.

"You're leaving on the same ship?" said Caleb, confused. "How can that be? You lived fifty years before my time?"

"I don't know? Maybe we will change ships at another port."

"That makes sense," said Caleb, smiling again.

The men grew silent. Then they looked up from the letters and concentrated on me. "What are we going to do about you?" asked Woodgate.

"I will manage on my own," I said, shrugging off their concern; though, in reality, I held back tears.

"Let's walk to Trent's house, he'll have to put you on our ship," said Caleb.

"Yes," agreed Woodgate.

"I can fend for myself," I said dismissively.

"No," insisted Woodgate. "It's decided. We'll go to Trent's house, first thing."

But Trent Cepulinski was not home. Woodgate rang the bell again and again, and we waited. Trent never answered his door.

"He's probably down at the dock," Caleb suggested.

When we reached the dock, sailors carried trunks and supplies onto a majestic ship. The townspeople, dressed in their Sunday best, milled around, hugging each other and exchanging pleasantries.

"Look!" said Caleb. "It's the *Jupiter Sunset*." Caleb pointed to the inscription on the stern of the ship. The golden inscription—the cursive "J" and the "UN" that swam into the letters, "IPER" should have registered immediately for me, but this was a whirling moment of stress and anxiety. My only friends on this island, seemingly in this world, were about to sail away, never to be seen again. No, I must admit, it wasn't until much later that I made the connection between that inscription and the one on the wooden flotsam that saved my life after my fall from the *Bonhomme Richard*.

"Eleven-Twenty," said Woodgate, peering at his new gold watch.

Caleb glanced at me. I could read sadness in his eyes, which were slightly magnified by his spectacles.

"This isn't right!" Caleb said. "Where is Trent? We have to find him." Caleb twisted his head left and right to search the dock.

"I will manage, Caleb."

"No, you won't!" said Caleb. "It's not right. You're with us."

Caleb balanced on his tiptoes in an attempt to see over the multitude, while Woodgate excused himself and moved toward the ship.

"Remember, last night, we saw that fence with the no trespassing sign—you know, the one that we passed coming back from the dinner behind the church?" I said, knowing that this was an awkward time to broach the subject. But the ship—the *Juniper Sunset*—rocking and bobbing in its slip, attached to a gangway, upon which men and women would soon walk along in single file and then

176

disappear into the belly of the ship, served as a forceful reminder that time was limited, Caleb would soon be gone—forever. In my mind, it was now or never.

Caleb exhaled, obviously frustrated by his inability to track down Cepulinski. "Fence? What fence?"

"You did not see it? Up there, to the left of the church." I pointed along the pathway that hugged the harbor, beyond Cepulinski's house.

"I don't know—yes, I think so. What about it?" Caleb was hopping up and down, trying to see over see over the thickening crowd, desperately searching for Cepulinski.

"I climbed over that fence last night, after you and Woodgate went to be, and I found another shipyard—a wharf much like this one—abandoned."

The *Juniper Sunset* would board and depart within the half hour, a time constraint that unnerved Caleb. I heard him swear under his breath as he stamped his feet on the ground. I wondered if he were actually listening to what I was saying. Then he shook his head with disappointment, and said, "Another shipyard? So what?"

"You remember the letter from the French woman?"

Caleb ceased fidgeting and locked his eyes on mine. "What about her?"

"Remember that she wrote about choosing the ship she would return on?"

"In her dreams, yes. She dreamed that she would have to choose a ship."

"Yes, and one ship would bring her home, the other . . ."

"I'm not following you?" Caleb interrupted.

"It is simple. We—you, me, Woodgate—have not been offered a choice. You've been told what ship you are to board. I haven't been given . . ."

A great horn sounded, effecting an immense change in the crowd: the already bustling dockside increased its movement, suddenly swelling and attenuating like the lungs of a great beast, and then almost if by design, organizing itself into a serpentine queue in front of the gangplank attached to the *Juniper Sunset*. A tall gaunt man, in a black uniform, collected notes of embarkation (written, notably, on the same stationery as the letters held by Woodgate and Caleb). He scanned the letters with his eyes, nodded approvingly, and then moved aside to allow each traveler room to process along the gangplank.

Woodgate suddenly appeared next to me, red-faced and perspiring. "The cadaverous bugger!"

"What?" Caleb said.

"That cadaverous toad accepting tickets over there." Woodgate pointed to the man in black. "I just spoke with him, implored him to allow Prescott to board with us. Every question I posed received the same automaton response, 'No letter, no entry. No letter, no entry.' I'd like to punch that satanic smirk off of his face," said Woodgate peering over his shoulder at the man. "The ignominious imp."

"I suppose this is it," I said, as the man in black shouted, "Last call! Last call to board!"

Woodgate shrugged his shoulder. "Prescott," he said offering me his hand. "I'm afraid that it is impossible." We shook hands. "It has been a great joy getting to know you over the past couple of days. I am all the better for it."

"Likewise," I said.

The line in front of the man in black had dwindled greatly.

Woodgate gently rested his hand on Caleb's right shoulder. "We have to go."

"But what about Prescott? We can't leave him?"

"We can't stay here!" said Woodgate, patting him vigorously on the shoulder. "Get a grip. We have people to return to—home."

Woodgate returned his attention to me, "You'll straighten this all out, right, Prescott?"

"Yes, sir, I . . ."

"You see," said Woodgate. "And he'll board a ship later today or tomorrow."

"I'm not going without him," said Caleb, scanning the area for Cepulinski. "That little rat can't do this to him."

"You're talking nonsense. You've been on this dismal island longer than all of us. You need to go home." Woodgate grimaced and ran his hand through his hair.

Caleb peered down at me. He was clearly exasperated.

"Please, Caleb," I said.

"What?"

"He is correct. You cannot risk it. If you stay behind, you could lose your opportunity to go home."

The last person in line handed his letter to the man in the black uniform.

"All aboard! Last chance—all aboard the Jupiter Sunset!" the man called as he rang a silver hand bell.

"Come on, Caleb," said Woodgate, tugging at his upper arm.

Caleb looked at the ship and then at me.

"Go," I said. "Please go."

Caleb exhaled, defeated.

"Letters?" I studied the gaunt face on the man in the black uniform. His pronounced orbital sockets made his sunken eyes look like coals encircled in soot. The man's toothy mouth did give the indication of a smirk, and his strange nose, it was so small that it seemed to not be there at all.

Woodgate tendered his letter, stepped onto the gangway, and turned to watch Caleb reluctantly present his letter. As the man examined it, Caleb turned to me and shook my hand. "You're a great friend, Prescott. I'll never forget all you've done for me."

"All I have done?" I said, tears coursing down my cheeks. "It is you who should be thanked for opening my eyes."

Caleb leaned down and gave me a bear hug and then, a little embarrassed by this show of affection, awkwardly jumped onto the gangway.

Woodgate and Caleb climbed to the main deck and then blended in with the multitude. Eager to position myself for a clear

179

view of the ship's departure, I pressed my diminutive frame through small openings in the throng and then settled in a spot against the dock railing.

The crew of the *Juniper Sunset*, a sorry squad of sailors, malnourished in appearance, wan faces, downtrodden, ragged, and funereal in their movements, worked at sliding the gangway away from the ship, unceremoniously lifting several massive ropes from posts, and then hoisting the main sails.

I clearly remember the canvas sails immediately billowed in the wind, a mysterious current of air that I did not feel on the ground, and then the ship eased out of the slip.

I scanned the stern for Caleb and Woodgate, but they did not reveal themselves to me.

"Bon voyage, my friends," I said quietly. "Bon voyage and goodbye."

Chapter Thirty-Eight
INTUITION AND INGENUITY

THE *JUPITER SUNSET* PITCHED AND ROLLED as it moved beyond the serene waters in the cove to the open sea. I watched its sails grow smaller and smaller in the distance, and I mourned the fact that I would never again see my new friends, especially Caleb. The throng on the wharf did not disperse when the top of the *Jupiter Sunset's* main mast sank below the horizon. Instead, it seemed to swell, as space became a premium and my chest pressed up against the railing.

I felt a soft hand on my wrist. I followed the arm up to white shoulders on which chestnut-brown hair fell. Then I beheld the face: white skin, red-pouted lips, and ocean blue eyes.

"Melanie!" I shouted.

"Shh!" she uttered, and then she looked around before leaning down and bringing her lips to my ear, "I need to talk to you."

"All right. About what?" I said into her ear.

"Not here," she said, and then she handed me a small screw of paper.

I opened the paper, which she had folded several times, and read the message.

Prescott,
Things are not what they seem. Meet me in the Charlie Horse Tavern at 1 O'clock. Do not return to the Sparrow Inn and do not seek the Clerk of the Works again.
Yours Kindly,
Melanie Simpson

"What?" I said, and quickly turned to look at Melanie, but she was gone. In her place stood a frumpy, middle-aged woman in a yellow wrap-around gown.

I believe something inside of me snapped at that moment. I was tired of being a pawn to some unknown players, jostled around from place-to-place without as much as a rational explanation. I jammed the paper in my front trouser pocket and wedged my way through the crowd.

When I pierced the masses and separated myself from the noise and pandemonium, I had only one thought in mind: return to my home on the plateau.

I increased my walking pace to a slow jog, passing house after uniform gray house. I bumped into several strollers, but did not slow to offer my apologies. In five minutes I was where the village ended and the sandy precipitous path began. I skipped down the three steps and began striding up the hill. The sun burned now. I continued walking, though more slowly than before, and had to constantly wipe the sweat from my forehead and eyes.

When I reached the granite steps, I turned around for a moment to look down at the village and was horrified to see that all those who had been standing on the dock with me were now standing in the sand in front of the entrance to the boardwalk. Foremost in the crowd stood Melanie—her white dress wavered like hot air in the distance—and next to her, Trent Cepulinski. Yes, the self-proclaimed Clerk of The Works stood there, his arms crossed, gazing up at me. None in the crowd moved.

I quickly turned and began ascending the uneven steps. I climbed and climbed, sweating, breathing hard, and spitting the excess saliva that my body produced as a result of the exercise. My lungs heaving, I stopped and sat upon a step. The villagers remained an unmoving mass of multicolor. They simply continued to watch my progress as I ascended the hillside. What did they want? Why did they stare at me so? I did not want to stay around to find out, as I felt more and more now that I had escaped horrible consequences. The dappled colors of Cepulinski's minions coupled with the gray roofs in the village that appeared from this height like seagull feathers strewn on a beach could have been a pleasant harlequin view, but did not resonate in an artistic way for me at that moment.

When I had regained normal breathing, I renewed my ascent, though I did not move as quickly as before, confident that there was ample distance between the villagers and me to preclude them from overtaking or capturing me.

My legs were wobbly when I stood on the marble stoop in front of the craggy rock surface of the mountain. At first I casually searched for the door that I had entered through the day before, but it was indiscernible in the rock, and I saw no handle or knob to use to open it. My anxiety flared, as I began to frantically search the rough surface for a lever, or a secret handle, or a crack, but all was in vain. Nearing delirium, wanting to pull my own hair out of my head, I turned my body away from the rough mount, slumped against its rocky surface, and let out a sigh of frustration.

Movement.

The stippled mass below began rearranging its composition, reorganizing itself into an ordered column. The villagers were now climbing the hill. They were coming after me!

I panicked. I began tugging madly on the rocky skin of the mountain. I kicked. I barreled my shoulder into the side, but the door remained invisible. I did not even detect hollowness.

The villagers now walked single file up the trail. There was no indication of a need to rush, no desperation in their ascent. Still, intuition told me that they meant me harm, that this was an angry mob, not a welcoming party.

"There must be a way!" I shouted to myself. "Think!"

I noticed a stone about the size of a horse's head on the ground. I strained to pick it up—but managed to lift it only as high as my knees. I called out, "One, two, three!" and then lobbed it against the craggy mountainside. The rock scraped harmlessly against the mountain and then smashed down on the marble floor and broke in two.

I peered over my shoulder: the villagers had reached the granite steps.

I picked up the smaller of the two pieces of the stone and found I could wield it fairly easily. But what could I smash it against? It was not as if I were breaking glass.

Glass!

I remembered the glass surface against the outside wall of the great hall. I had seen light shining through cascading water and then through the glass, which created the flickering shadows throughout the great hall. I looked to my left and realized there was a small ledge that I could climb out upon. I threw up the stone and then pulled myself onto the ledge.

Once atop of the ledge, I picked up the stone and, with my back to the mountain, began sliding my feet along the ledge, which led me around to the left side of the volcanic mountain. I looked downward and left to gauge the villagers' progress: They were now moving faster; running in single file, like a long line of colorful insects, along the granite stairway.

I continued to edge my way along the side of the mountain. The path widened twenty-five feet from where I started. I could walk with my right shoulder to the mountainside. The ledge rose slightly, and then I spied great crevices in the mountainside. Ducking into one narrow crevice I perceived the glinting of glass.

I moved along the ledge until I found a crevice big enough to fit my body inside. I heaved the stone in the crevice, and then dragged myself in, my chest and stomach brushing against the jagged rock. I felt like an insect, a beetle, using my arms as feelers, pushing ahead the stone and then crawling blindly toward it. This continued for more than five minutes, until when I shoved the stone ahead, I heard it hit a surface that did not sound like rock. I quickly crept up to the stone and then felt beyond it. My hand hit a flat, smooth surface that was cold to the touch.

I made a fist and knocked against it. The knocking produced a resonant sound consistent with what I expected from glass. Wasting no time, I pulled back a little, grasped the stone, and then threw it with all my might into the glass surface. The glass made a terrific noise upon contact with the stone, reverberating like a giant gong, but did not break.

I tried this same method again and again, to no avail. I concluded that I was not throwing the stone fast enough to break the thick glass.

I could hear voices consistent with what I once heard during the riots in Boston. This was a mob, led by a hangman, angry and desperate, tasting blood—my blood.

"My arms are not strong enough," I said, censuring myself.

Then an idea came to me. I placed the stone a few feet from the glass and crawled back several feet. Then, knowing that I could produce more force with my legs, I lay on my back, pulled my legs up to my chest, and then used my feet to push the stone with as much force as I could possibly exert.

Crash!

The glass shattered into shards of what seemed like a million pieces. Still on my back, I worked my way toward the opening I had created in the glass and managed to crab-crawl through without cutting myself on the needle-like splinters.

The crevice opened to a great height, which allowed me to stand and look around. I discovered a new obstacle: a great rushing waterfall emerging from the darkness above. I thought back to yesterday when I stood inside the great hall looking at the glass wall. I had seen light intermingled with the motion of water; therefore, I concluded almost immediately that there should be another glass pane beyond the waterfall.

I searched the ground and, spying the stone, quickly picked it up and walked to the right, where I met with a dead end. I then turned and walked left until I perceived a slight incline. I slid my feet a few inches at a time up the incline, edging my way around the waterfall. There, I discovered another pane of glass.

I raised the stone above my head, bent my knees, and then heaved the stone, grunting loudly with the effort. The glass surface exploded inward, and I immediately sensed a great breeze rushing against my face, as the warm volcanic air from within escaped.

Though still in shadow, I saw rays of light inside, falling from the open ceiling. I gingerly stepped over the jagged shards of glass and into the room, eventually walking into the light of the great hall. The water fountain and its twin jets burbled in the distance, and to my right I saw the mirrored wall where Caleb, Woodgate, and I stood yesterday. A pang of sadness poked at my insides every time I thought of Caleb. I missed his companionship.

I paid little mind to the predatory villagers outside, but I should have, because as I strolled lazily through the archway into the portico, I heard a loud thud and the roar of a bloodthirsty crowd. I snapped my head over my left shoulder and saw Cepulinski standing beneath the opened portal.

I ran.

And as I did, I am quite certain it was Cepulinski who screamed, "NO!"

The portico was a blur in my peripheral vision. I skipped several steps as I ascended the marble steps up into the cave. Inside the cave, in pitch dark, I crashed into a wall on two or three occasions, cutting my knee in the process. At the turn I jogged, kicking my feet out forward as I did so that I might feel an obstacle and make adjustments to avoid hitting it with my head.

Soon I was running down the spiraling walkway, laboring for breath, but no burning of the lungs could convince me to slow down. I was running on pure adrenaline—it pumped in my veins, making my muscles twitch with surprising speed.

At the mouth of the cave, I stopped and glanced up. I saw nothing, but, because I breathed so heavily, I could hear nothing above my panting. I walked briskly now, in an attempt to regain regular respiration, and listened, constantly listened.

But all was silent.

When I reached the hard-packed dirt path beyond the boardwalk, I felt safe. I passed Caleb's birthstone, where he had laughed so merrily yesterday, and relived many of the memories of our time together on the island. I imagined him as I saw him on the first day, when he mistook me for an actor. I pictured him gathering dodos in my coat in front of a red sunset. I thought of him constructing his bench and then lying on it, his hands behind his head and a pompous smirk on his face.

All images never to be seen again.

Pushing my way through the spiraled vines, I happily entered the sunny beach and then fell back into the sand. My legs and hands trembled from the exercise. My lungs wheezed as I breathed. My hair on my head gathered in stringy clumps of dried sweat.

After a ten-minute rest, standing up was difficult because my muscles had stiffened. I gazed over at the two stone statues and a flash of insight stroked through me. I moved closer and studied the faces on the statues. I saw a new familiarity in the long noses, the impish smiles, and the small frames.

"Cepulinski," I said aloud. There was some resemblance to the little old man—the Clerk of the Works—but some features did not match. Trent had no hair, and these statues had curly masses of hair that hugged their skulls like a helmet. Trent wore spectacles, which were not present on the end of the long granite noses.

More peculiar than the notion that these statues likely represented a young Trent Cepulinski was that the sculptures seemed to have aged overnight. They were covered in thin surface cracks, like spider webs, and the stone appeared brittle, fragile. To my great surprise I reached over and touched the ear of one statue and it turned to dust in my hand.

"Strange," I whispered to myself.

As I approached the cliff below the plateau, I noticed smoke rising from the area I called home. I watched the black smoke waft out above the sea and disappear behind a wall of approaching thunderheads. I knew it could not be yesterday's fire still burning. Caleb had squelched the fire by kicking sand onto it before we left.

Horrifying thoughts raced across my mind. Could it be the villagers—the mob? Are Cepulinski and his cohorts lying in wait for me?

Eager to hide myself from view, I raced to the edge of the beach, where the sand meets the verdant jungle. In the shade of a great palm, my mind ran a list of other possible reasons for the fire upon the plateau. Perhaps Woodgate and Caleb had returned? Maybe we do live outside of time and this is my first day on the island and I will again meet Caleb? Perhaps the Misty Village experience never occurred?

I moved behind a great boulder, peering up at the plateau. The rational part of my brain desperately searched for the safest and most reasonable thing to do next.

A human shape.

I saw a figure, short in stature, standing by the edge of the cliff with his arms akimbo, looking down at the sea.

"Who can that be?" I whispered.

I ducked my head and then sat in the sand behind the boulder. "I'll soon find out," I stated emphatically, "because I am going up there to reclaim my home."

I stole another quick look and the figure was gone from view.

"Time to work on a cogent plan of approach."

Chapter Thirty-Nine
ENLIGHTENMENT

WHAT IS THE WORST THING THAT could happen to me? I asked myself this, as I sat cowering behind that boulder. The worst thing would be for me to die, I decided. But I was still not convinced that I was alive in the first place. After all, had I not seen the sailors the day before carrying trunks with "*U.S.S. Triumph*" emblazoned on them? And did I not learn that the Triumph sank on its maiden voyage, killing hundreds of its passengers? Well, if the *U.S.S. Triumph* sank, then why was it docked at Misty Village? A rational person might surmise that the ship and its passengers miraculously survived somehow. But I know enough about what happened immediately before Caleb, Woodgate, and I arrived on this island to build an argument that defies and resists such natural logic.

The villagers had followed me out of Misty Village, led by Trent Cepulinski. How do I know they meant me harm? I do not know for certain, but I sensed it. It was a matter of instinct. They raced toward me like a pack of predators upon catching the scent of a wounded animal. When the cave door did not open, I became that wounded animal—and the hunt was on.

But here, on the other side of the island, I should have felt safe, except that the notion that someone—some small figure—now occupied my camp bothered and frightened me. Cepulinski's visage streaked across my consciousness like heat lightning.

Peeking over the boulder, I noticed that the fire had petered out; it gave off only traces of smoke. Great strokes of lightning sizzled above the sea, and sudden gusts of wind blew inland, prefiguring an approaching storm. I was nauseated from dehydration and insufficient nourishment. I realized I could not remain on the beach tonight, especially in this condition and with a storm approaching.

I slapped my knees, rebuked my cowardice, and then stood up straight. I would not give up my home without a fight, so I began marching down the beach, past the sheer cliffs below the plateau, and up the precipitous sandy path. At the pinnacle, I could see Caleb's hooch, the campfire, and Caleb's bench, but no human figure.

It was not until I reached the campfire that I saw a pair of small, white feet protruding from the hooch.

"Who goes there?" I yelled in a deep voice.

The feet withdrew and then I saw blonde curly hair, followed by white shoulders, as a young boy crawled out. "It's me," he said in a high voice. "I go here."

The boy wore yellow short pants, no shirt, and carried a rectangular black box on a strap around his neck. I deduced that he was a couple of years younger than me, perhaps 10 years of age.

He then stood up and smiled.

"And who are you?"

"Tommy," he said. "Tommy Snyder."

"Are you aware that you are sleeping in my bed, Tommy Snyder?"

"No . . . and yes," he said.

"Explain yourself."

"No, I did not know it was your bed," he said, looking at his feet. "Yes, I knew the bed belonged to somebody."

"Where are you from?"

"Canada—Toronto," he said.

"Are you alone?"

"Yes."

I walked over and peered into the empty hooch. "How did you get here?"

"I walked."

"No, Tommy. Where were you before you came to this island?"

"I was in a plane. But it didn't land here. It was a two-passenger Cessna and my father was the pilot. The engines stalled and we crashed into . . . into the sea."

"Come over here," I said, in a gentle voice.

The boy obeyed and stopped in front of me. I offered him my hand, which his tiny hand latched onto, and I introduced myself. Up close, I realized that I dwarfed this boy in height and weight.

"It is nice to meet you, Tommy," I said, trying to demonstrate kindness, civility. "I am Prescott Fielding."

The distant boom of thunder sounded, and soon rain fell in torrents. Tommy and I took shelter beneath the tarpaulin in the hooch. There I explained to the boy about this side of the island, mostly geographical information that included where to get drinking water and where to get berries and bananas.

Within an hour's time, I learned more about how Tommy arrived on the island. Tommy explained that the plane his father piloted malfunctioned and made a crash landing in the ocean. Upon impact, Tommy perceived a streak of light, a blinding flash, and then the next thing he knew, he was facedown on the beach below the plateau. Tommy assumed that he had washed ashore, but I knew better. Suddenly rivulets of tears rolled down his cheeks, as he explained that he doubted his father survived the crash.

The late afternoon was dark, and the storm continued its frenzy, as great gusts of wind threatened to rip the plastic roof from the hooch. Tommy shivered in the wind, so I wrapped my arms around him to warm and comfort him. He sniffled from time to time, though, as he continued crying.

To cheer him up, I recounted stories about Caleb and Woodgate. I chuckled as I spoke of how Woodgate insisted on taking his trousers off yesterday as he walked along the sand. Tommy did not join me in my laughter, and I didn't blame him, because it was the visual image, not my description, that stirred hilarity in me.

When the storm abated, I suggested that we venture out to gather food and water. As I spoke these words, I heard a strange cheeping sound emanating from Tommy's body.

"What is that?"

"What?" he said.

"That high-pitched peeping sound!"

191

"Oh, that. It's just my computer." He lifted the rectangular black box that he carried on a strap around his neck.

"What is a computer?"

"You don't know what a computer is?"

"They do not have them where I come from."

"Where do you come from—Mars?"

"No, I come from a time long ago when people did not have computers or planes or trains or tanks." I searched my memory for other modern devices that Caleb had told me about, but found that I had exhausted my list.

Tommy pressed his thumbs against the computer, which now tooted and peeped more frequently.

"What's your full name again?" he asked.

I told him, and he began madly punching buttons on this computer.

"What year was it when you and your father flew in the plane?" I said, sorry to bring up the subject of his father.

"What do you mean?" Tommy asked, looking up at me and ceasing to tap his fingers on the computer.

"Was it 1968!" I said, remembering the year when Caleb arrived.

"1968?" Tommy said in a voice of astonishment. "I wasn't born in 1968! My father wasn't born in 1968! It was 2031. Why, when were you born?"

"Oh," I said chuckling. "A long time before 1968."

"What?" he said. "How can that be?"

"I guess I look young for my age," I explained.

"Before 1968?" Tommy said doubtfully. "Wow! You're kind of old, huh?"

"Yes; you could say so."

"No, nothing in here about you. There are other Prescott Fieldings, but none that looks like you," Tommy said, looking up from his computer.

"What do you mean?"

"I ran a search on your name, but nothing came up."

"That machine tells you about people?"

"It will tell you about most anything," said Tommy.

"What does it say about Caleb Thompson of the United States Marine Corps?"

Tommy rapidly pressed buttons and then stared at the bluish screen.

"Did he fight in the Vietnam War?" Tommy asked.

"Yes! Yes! That is he. What does it tell you?" I leaned over to gaze at the screen. There, seemingly by magic, was an image of Caleb. "That is Caleb! Ha-ha! I never thought I would see your face again. Can I talk to him?"

"No, you can't talk to him. It's a digitized rendering of an old photograph," said Tommy.

"What does it all mean?"

Tommy caused the picture to rise and disappear. Then, English words appeared in a neat and uniform arrangement that was very easy to read.

"It says here that he was pronounced dead on January 4th, 1969, in Da Nang, Vietnam."

"What!" I said, shrieking. "That cannot be true." But it was true; I read it with my own eyes. I learned that Caleb was "Missing in Action" for eight weeks before officials found his body floating in a rice paddy, near Hill 19.

Chills ran down my spine when I realized that Caleb, my dear friend Caleb, had been on this island 60 days—about eight weeks!— before sailing out of Misty Village today. This time coincidence horrified me.

"What about Julian Woodgate?" I said, knowing that he had spent three days on the island. "Please place his name in that thing; I would like to learn what happened to him."

Tommy tapped at the computer keyboard like a woodpecker on the flank of a tree. "It is showing several Julian Woodgates. What else can you tell me?"

"I know he is from England . . . and he fought in World War One!"

"Okay," Tommy said, punching more buttons. "Is this your man?" Tommy lifted the computer to my face, and there, in hues of blacks, grays and whites, was Woodgate as I remembered him.

"That is he!" I said. "What does it tell you about him?"

"I hate to break it to you," Tommy said. "But he's dead too."

"When?" I said, impatiently. "When did he die?"

"July 17th, 1916—in a shell attack," said Tommy. "They recovered his remains three days after the attack, and buried him in High Wood Cemetery."

Chapter Forty
OBLIVION

THE RECENT STORM A DISTANT MEMORY, the jungle around us simmered in the early evening sun, which hung, blood red, in the turquoise sky. Tommy, his computer strapped around his neck, smiled kindly at me, completely ignorant of his new reality on this island, this oblivion. At that moment, despite tortuous thoughts tearing at the gray matter in my head, I forced myself to maintain a genial expression, and leaned over and patted the bright-eyed boy on the shoulder.

Wisps of clouds scudded by in the distance, and I pointed out to Tommy that the gray area near the horizon was a small rainstorm over the ocean. I believe I even told him several stories about storms that I encountered while sailing on the *Bonhomme Richard*. My verbal facility has never once failed me in my life, and it did not fail me then, for I continued regaling my new friend with stories of the sea while my mind added, measured, analyzed, overturned, dissected, and pulverized every conversation, every sight, and every moment of the last twenty-four hours. And like metal filings to a magnet, every thought ended its journey with two mental images: the digitized pictures of Caleb and Woodgate that I saw on Tommy's computer.

The storm had passed, and the darkness of night would envelope us soon, so I decided to take a walk and gather some fresh water and food before retiring for the evening, but in truth I wished to be alone with my thoughts. When I suggested to Tommy that he remain behind at the camp, he exclaimed, "You're not leaving me up here all alone!"

"Am I not?" I said, surprised by his tone of voice.

"What are you nuts?" he said, standing up. "This island gives me the creeps. Did you see those statues on the beach?"

He obviously spoke of the statues that I now believed represented Trent Cepulinski.

"Yes, I have. What about them?"

"I don't know," said Tommy, now walking along side of me, as we headed down the hill. "That was one of the first things I saw when I got here. It made me feel funny."

"Funny?"

"Yeah. You know, as in strange."

"Strange? How so?"

"I don't know. Like that story Hansel and Gretel. You know that one?"

"I do not."

"Well, in the story, these two starving kids—Hansel and Gretel—find a house made of gingerbread in the forest, and they're attracted to it and begin eating it, but they don't know that inside the house lives a witch who eats children."

I stopped walking and turned to this bright boy. "And?"

"And what?"

"How does that relate to the statues?"

"I don't know? I guess I felt strange, as if part of me wanted to get closer to the statues, but something inside of me said, 'It's just a house made of gingerbread.'"

I smiled at my intelligent friend, and as I did, I felt my eyes well up with tears, and then I reached over and tousled Tommy's hair. "You are very perceptive."

"What do you mean?" asked Tommy, who then moved to a flat stone on the side of the path and sat down to tie his shoe. The broad smile on his face assured me that he was clearly pleased with my praise.

I sat next to him. "I suppose . . . well . . . ." Tommy peered up at me with great curiosity, his mouth slightly ajar, his blue eyes squinting. "I felt the very same thing that you felt when I first saw those statues." I looked away in the direction of the sun, which was now low in the sky and would, within an hour, begin to submerge into the ocean. "As a matter of fact, my suspicions were confirmed last night."

"Confirmed? What do you mean?"

"Tommy, that computer," I said pointing to the box strapped around his neck. "Do me a favor and enter another name. I am curious."

Tommy pulled the strap over his head, flipped the cover, and a bluish light illuminated his face. "What name?"

"Trent Cepulinski."

"Cepulinski? What kind of a name is that? How do you spell it?"

I wasn't certain about the spelling, but after a few tries, Cepulinski's little rat face appeared on the screen. Interestingly enough, in that picture Cepulinski had a great mass of curly brown hair and he did not wear spectacles.

"That is he! What does it say?" I leaned in close to Tommy.

"Born in St. Paul, Minnesota on April 20th, 1949. Disappeared on March 11th, 2002. Assumed dead."

"Why am I not surprised?" I stood up and walked a few paces away from Tommy.

"Hey, this guy was bad news!" said Tommy.

"What?"

"War Criminal and Murderer Vanishes. That's what the headline says." Tommy's eyes raced across the digital text. "He was in the Vietnam War. He left his platoon and captured a whole Vietnamese village. He was a ruthless killer. He terrorized the poor Vietnamese civilians, murdered twenty of them before he was captured." Tommy's eyes showed the whites around his pupils.

"This is insanity."

"Speaking of insanity," said Tommy, engrossed in the story of Cepulinski. "This guy spent more than a decade in a sanitarium. Check out this: 'Cepulinski was released from the Broodmare Hospital in 1980. He married soon after, fathered a child, worked as a janitor, and lived a quiet existence in a suburb outside of Boston.' This part is boring. Let's see," Tommy scanned the screen. "Aha! 'In the fall of 2002, neighbors complained of a strong smell emanating from his house. Police later discovered three dead bodies in an old refrigerator in his garage. Among the dead were his wife and 20-year-old daughter—Melanie was her name."

I raced over to Tommy's side. "Does it show Melanie's likeness?"

Tommy pressed a few buttons and then a beautiful, auburn-haired girl appeared—Melanie Simpson.

"Do you know her too?"

"Yes."

"Do you know anybody who is still alive?"

"I know you," I said, without realizing the ponderous irony in that statement.

Tommy made the screen roll, and I watched Melanie's face disappear into the top of the computer.

"You know Cepulinski too?"

"Yes, unfortunately," I said somberly.

"He was a slippery dude. It says here that after his killing spree, he jumped off the Tobin Bridge, in Boston. They never recovered his body. Maybe? No," said Tommy, quickly changing directions. "No, he didn't fake his death. There were eyewitnesses that saw him jump. It says here that no human could survive such a fall."

"What about Melanie?"

"Yuck!" said Tommy. "Trust me, you don't want to know."

"What?"

"That's wicked nasty!"

"What!"

"Your friend Cepulinski—"

"He is not my friend!" I interrupted.

"Well, that Cepulinski cut out his daughter's heart and preserved it in a jar that he kept in his house. The police never recovered the rest of her body."

"How can that be?" I said, taking a deep breath and picturing the young girl as she stood on the hillside when Caleb, Woodgate, and I first met her.

Then I remembered the dream I had last night.

I dreamt I saw Melanie, bathed in white light, walking toward me but never gaining ground . . . and what had I heard the whole time? A heartbeat!

"The Melanie I knew . . . the Melanie I knew, she had a heart— I'm certain of it." I peered out at the ocean. The cool sea breeze caressed my face.

Perhaps Melanie had planned to help me after all.

I quickly searched my pockets to retrieve her short note, and when I reached into my waistcoat pocket, instead of a folded paper, I withdrew a small, pink envelope. "This is curious."

"What?" asked Tommy, but I ignored him and hurriedly opened the envelope and extracted a folded piece of stationery.

Dear Prescott Fielding,

I placed this note in your pocket, but my hope is that it will not be necessary, as I plan to speak with you in person. But if that cannot be, I offer you these hastily scribbled words.

Yesterday, when I met you on the hillside, I was performing my duty of singing arias to attract the newly arrived—to help convince them to walk through the cave door. But, as I do every day, I was also searching for a way to escape back through the cave.

Ever since Trent Cepulinski, my father, gained control of Misty Village, no one has ever returned through that door. But I have long believed that if someone can pass back through the cave door and escape from Misty Village, my father's reign of terror will end.

You were not on my father's list, and no one can figure out why, especially my father. Perhaps you are not supposed to be on this island, and that worries my father. You cannot be like the other souls on this island. Your situation is different. I know this because my father would have placed you on the Juniper Sunset with your friends if he could have. But he could not, which caused him such fits that he spent the entire morning on his knees in the chapel.

I don't know what brought you here, but in my mind you're here to end the terror.

There was a time when some ships carried the souls back home. I hope and pray, against my father's wishes, that day will come again soon.

God be with you,

Melanie Simpson

Several silent minutes slipped by.

I inhaled deeply and allowed my mind to wander, while studying the deep red circle of the sun. I had arrived at the island by a means much different from Caleb, Woodgate, and Tommy. They arrived in a sudden flash, as if traveling at the speed of light. I grasped on to a piece of flotsam . . . That was it! Had a piece of the *Juniper Sunset* carried me into this oblivion?

Looking through my eyelashes at the sun, a halo formed and I immediately thought of Caleb. I heard the sequent breathing of the tide as it crashed, rushed forward, and then retreated. I heard the gulls, winging across the beach in search of food, calling out in their characteristic sharp tones. My ears perceived all the noises of the living, breathing island. But would my ears ever perceive the sound of the sun? Would my ship ever come in? Would I ever find all the answers?

Suddenly mind raced back along the Boston wharf, to that day in the alley when I watched the fat man moving thimbles over a board resting on his lap. He used dexterity and practiced sleight of hand to cheat honest merchants out of their money. None ever had a chance to win. It was a swindle, a ruse.

Was this island simply a deadly version of a thimblerig game? Were all the lost souls who stumbled upon this verdant isle merely marionettes—puppets strung along by a madman? Had they all entered into a bet that they could never win? Bet their souls in a game—a thimblerig game?

Was there a time—a time before Cepulinski— when those ships in that abandoned Misty Village shipyard were used to carry souls home?

I turned slowly, and then looked down at Tommy, into those gentle blue eyes.

"Here," I said, offering him my hand, which he grasped, and then I pulled him into a standing position. I placed my arm around his shoulder and we began walking down the path. There would be a day when I would explain to Tommy what I knew about this island, and I would tell him that I believed his father was alive (for, if he were not alive, he would be here, I concluded). Of course, the notion that Caleb, Woodgate, and I had buried his father several nights ago suddenly gripped and horrified me.

I analyzed my own fate. In my former life, God had never blessed me with a younger brother; yet, here and now I had Tommy, someone who I would grow to love and cherish as a brother.

We continued walking along the sandy beach without speaking, until Tommy exclaimed, "Look!" He pointed at two curious golden objects glinting in the late afternoon sunlight. The objects were in the same location as the statues of Cepulinski, which caused my heart to triple its rate. Tommy excitedly ran ahead, despite my call for him to wait. Fearful of losing my new companion to these mysterious golden idols, I raced after him.

When I reached Tommy, he stood a few feet in front of these shiny objects, his mouth agape, simply mesmerized. I immediately understood his captivation when I studied the shiny objects in the sand: two golden statues of a young man in a waistcoat, breeches, long stockings, and buckled sailor shoes. More curiously, the figure held a wrinkled piece of paper against its chest.

"Prescott. These statues. They look like you!"

After studying the face, I could not disagree. And when I searched behind for evidence of the Cepulinski statues, I found only pulverized granite.

"Prescott?"

"Yes?"

"What is this place?"

I drew up close to the boy and put my arm around him as we both continued to gaze at my likeness molded in what appeared to be solid gold.

"This place?" I said softly and sadly. "This place, my brother, is . . . oblivion."

"Oblivion?" he said, looking up at me with a confused expression.

"Oblivion," I confirmed, now patting him on the back and then tousling his hair. "But," I now smiled broadly and winked at him, "from now on, Tommy, you and I will call it our home."

THE END

ABOUT THE AUTHOR

Roger Whittlesey lives in Massachusetts with his wife Christy.

22891385R00110

Made in the USA
Lexington, KY
17 May 2013